Sweetest Kisses

Book Four in the Sprawling A Ranch Series

By

Anna Alexander

Small-town life fits Adam Maguire like a pair of favorite blue jeans, while Nicolette Fournier finds it as constricting as a straitjacket. But when this good ol' country boy and rock n roll princess come together, sparks fly hot enough to melt the icing on the delicious cakes in Nic's bake shop.

As the youngest of six brothers, nothing is more important to Adam than family, and he believes Nic would make a great addition to his. Only Nic is counting the days to when she has fulfilled familial obligations and can return to her life of open roads and adventure, leaving bad childhood memories in her rearview mirror. To make this free spirit his, Adam will have to pull out all of the stops to convince her that the only bed he wants to set his cowboy boots under are hers, and home wouldn't be complete without her Doc Martens beside them.

DEDICATION

To my family. Always.

And to the misfits who felt they never belonged. We are friends of the heart forever.

Find Anna Online

Website
annaalexander.net

Facebook
facebook.com/pages/Anna-Alexander/282170065189471

Twitter
twitter.com/AnnaWriter

Instagram
instagram.com/annam.alexander

Newsletter
http://eepurl.com/Q0tsz

Chapter One

THE DULCE VITA bakeshop held many a tempting treat, but Adam Maguire couldn't decide what he craved more: the row of chocolate cupcakes in the display case or the buns encased in tight denim that swayed enticingly in front of him from the top of a ladder.

His momma would smack him upside the head for leering, but he knew his fellow ranch hands would be at his side and enjoying the view. Well, the single guys, anyway. The attached ones would look then send him a wink before their girls caught them staring.

"I'll be right with you," the owner of the voluptuous backside said from over her shoulder as she replaced a light bulb in the ceiling.

"Take your time, darling," he drawled. "Take your time."

She snapped her head around to look down at him from her perch and her eyes widened for a second before returning to her work.

"You're a Maguire, aren't you?" she asked as she climbed down the ladder.

"Yes, ma'am. I'm Adam." He held out his hand. Partly to be polite, but mostly to have the chance to touch her.

At such close proximity, he detected her natural musk that was different from the sugary goodness of cake and icing surrounding him. Something darker, sexier. He swayed closer to catch a better sniff of her alluring fragrance.

She glanced at his hand for a few seconds before she looked up at him with the most unusual shade of brown eyes he had ever seen. They were a light caramel color made to look all the more exotic by her eye makeup. "Smoky eyes," that was what he remembered ghosts of girlfriends past call the look. But those girls always managed to look as if they had gotten into a fight and lost, while on this girl the heavy use of gray shadow and black eyeliner lent a hint of mystery, and he wanted to dive in and uncover her secrets.

"I'm Nic," she said and gripped his hand for a firm but brief shake.

"Is that short for Nicole?"

"Nicolette."

"Ooo...that sounds fancy. Nicolette," he trilled.

"Don't do that," she replied in a clipped tone then turned to gather the ladder. "It's just Nic."

When she turned, he noticed a bright red streak in the long strands of her ponytail. The back of her black T-shirt was shredded in a V-pattern and offered a tantalizing glimpse of the red strap of her bra. All she needed was a studded collar and fingerless gloves to complete her rocker look.

"Can I help you carry that?" he asked, remembering his manners even though he was distracted by her beauty.

"No, thanks. I am more than capable of carrying a ladder." She disappeared into a side room.

Touchy thing, wasn't she? "Didn't think you couldn't," he called out. "I was just being polite."

"Got it. Sorry. Didn't mean to throw decades of women's lib

in your face." She returned empty-handed and took a breath, resting her palms on the black and white tiled countertop. "Thank you for the offer, but I do not need your assistance. Liability issues and all of that. Your gentlemanly offer is appreciated."

Her formality made him smile. "Are you new in town?"

"New?" Her dark brows shot up in surprise. "No. I grew up here. In fact, I was in your brother Angus's class all through school."

"Really?" He rocked back on his heels. "He's only a few years older than me. Why don't I remember meeting you?"

"I don't think you and I have ever officially met, and I've never traveled in the same social circle as your brother."

"But still, I'd think our paths would've crossed at some time."

She shrugged. "They might have."

"And you've lived here your whole life?"

"Mostly. I lived in the city for a while, then Paris. I've been back in Mission for about a year."

"Paris? As in Paris, France?"

"Yep."

Whoa. He never knew anyone who'd been to another country before, let alone lived there. And in his opinion, Canada didn't count.

But Paris was miles away. Miles and miles of land, ocean, and mountains away. Paris required a plane to get to, and that thought alone made his stomach roll and chest ache with anxiety.

"And you lived there?" he asked incredulously.

The corner of her mouth kicked up. "Yes."

"For how long?"

"A few years."

"Really? So what brought you back?"

She shifted her weight and took a great interest in using a towel to wipe down the glass display case. "Stuff."

Ah. Another touchy subject.

"Do you miss it? Paris?"

"Every day," she replied softly and looked up at him with a gaze so forlorn, the ache in his chest returned. He swore he could taste her longing as if a big slab of the most bittersweet chocolate sat on his tongue.

"Oh. Adam. Hello." A woman appeared through the doorway to the kitchen with a flat stack of pink boxes in her hand. "I thought I heard someone out here."

"Ms. Devereux," he said with a tip of his cowboy hat.

"What brings you by today?" she asked.

"It's family dinner night at the old homestead. I want to surprise my mom and bring her that cheesecake she's done nothing but talk about for the last month. If I didn't know better, I'd think she'd run away and have an affair with it," he said with a wink.

Ms. Devereux chuckled. "Which cheesecake was she talking about?"

"She said it was like that Girl Scout cookie. The one with the coconut and caramel."

"Ah, yes." She snapped her fingers. "That has become our most popular treat. I think I may have one left in the back refrigerator."

"I'll go check," Nic volunteered and started for the kitchen.

"No, no." Ms. Devereux stopped her. "I'll go."

"I can get it, Aunt Jacqui. No problem."

Aunt Jacqui? Nic was Ms. Devereux's niece?

Adam narrowed his gaze and mentally nodded when he saw the family resemblance. Although Ms. Devereux had a good six to eight inches in height over her niece, they both had the same pointed noses, dimpled chins, and straight, dark hair, except for the streaks of gray in Ms. Devereux's and red in Nic's.

But it was in their features where any similarity began and ended. Ms. Devereux was not only tall, she was willowy as well, with a slim build, whereas Nic was all curves. She was built like an hourglass with plump hips and thighs, and a luscious rack he'd bet good money was all natural. She was just so soft-looking, he wanted to hug her close and luxuriate in all of that femaleness.

Perhaps his intrigue in the mysterious Nicolette stemmed from dating too many girls who changed diets as often as they changed their shoes, and spent as much time on their cellphones as they did looking in the mirror. That type of girl got boring real quick.

Girl. Hmmm. Maybe that was it. He had only dated girls and he was ready for a woman. A real woman. A woman who ate what she wanted, dressed the way she wanted, and got out into the world.

A woman like Nicolette.

"Nicolette," Ms. Devereux bit out before smiling in his direction. "I'll get the cake. You entertain our charming guest."

Before Nic had a chance to draw a breath, her aunt had disappeared into the back.

She sighed and turned back to him with a weak smile. "She'll be back with your order shortly. I'll ring you up down here."

"Take your time, Miss Devereux. I'm in no rush," he said as he moseyed toward the cash register.

"Fournier."

"What?"

"Fournier," Nic repeated. "My last name is Fournier. My mother and my aunt are sisters."

ANNA ALEXANDER

"Oh." He snapped his fingers. "Hey, I think I do remember your mama. I haven't seen her around town in years. Did she move away?"

Her breath hitched and a flash of distress darkened her eyes. "Something like that. Your total will be $32.78."

"Thirty-two dollars?" he exclaimed, about ready to choke on his spit. "It's a cheesecake."

"A really good cheesecake. Probably the best you'll ever have."

"What's it made out of? Gold? Diamonds?"

"Chèvre," she replied.

"I'm not familiar with that element."

A grin broke through her icy façade. "It's not an element, silly. It's a type of goat cheese." She pointed her finger at him as he curled his lip. "Don't make that face. Try it. If you don't want to have sex with that cake with the first taste, let me know and I'll refund your money."

Ah, she had to go and mention sex, didn't she? Now he couldn't stop picturing what she'd look like wearing nothing but cheesecake smeared all over her female bits.

"Wow. That is quite a claim. Now I'm looking forward to dessert tonight far more than I usually do." He pulled out his wallet and withdrew the cash. When she grasped the ends of the bills, he refused to let go, and when her confused gaze met his, he smiled. "How about next Friday you and me meet up and you can tell me more about your fancy ingredients."

Her brow crinkled. "I don't understand."

"Next Friday. You. Me. Go out."

"Out?" Blink-blink. Blink-blink. "Like on a date?"

"Yes."

"You're asking me out?"

"I'm trying to," he huffed, taking off his hat to swipe at the

6

sweat on his brow with the cuff of his shirt. The girl wasn't making this easy on him, was she? "Yes. I am asking you to go on a date with me."

"Why do you want to go out with me?"

He was starting to wonder the same thing, but he went with his gut that there was something about her he had to explore.

"For some reason, you," and here he held up his hands with his thumbs touching to form a frame, and gestured at her, "intrigue me. I find you smart, funny, and attractive. All things that are on the top of the list when it comes to women I'd like to date."

"Oh." Her lashes fluttered as if she were confused. "Oh. I'm not really sure what to say to that."

"To what part? The part where I asked you out, or the part where I said I'm attracted to you?"

"Yeah. Right there. The attracted part."

"Are you serious?" Now it was his turn to stare at her, dumbfounded. He shook his head and looked her up and down, stopping just short of licking his chops. "Girl, you've got it going on. I'm sure you have a line of men on speed dial waiting for you to call them up."

She raised her brow. "Now who's being serious? You do know where we live? No, I don't have men on speed dial. Unless you count the sheriff's office and fire department. I'm not your typical Mission girl."

"I know." His smile widened. "I think that's what I like best about you. So. What do you say? Next Friday? Eight o'clock?"

Nic's eyes widened. "Um..."

"Yes. She says yes," Ms. Devereux exclaimed from the entrance to the kitchen. Her smile was just as wide as the giant pink box in her hand.

"Aunt Jacqui—"

"You'll have so much fun," she gushed.

Nic turned to her aunt and gave her a wide-eyed, "What are you doing?" glare. "Aunt Jacqui, you know we're busy with other things next weekend." Her gaze drifted to the ceiling with purpose. The bakery was attached to the Devereux family home. Perhaps there was some domestic project they were working on in the living quarters.

"Pish-tosh. I've got it covered. Don't worry."

"But—"

Ms. Devereux held her hand in front of Nic's face to shush her and flashed Adam a big smile. "I expect to see you next Friday at eight o'clock, young man. And pick Nic up at the front of the house like a proper gentleman."

"Yes, ma'am." He tipped his hat at her. Sure, he would have liked it if Nic had jumped up and down with joy and shouted yes to his request for a date, but he sensed Nic didn't go out very often, at least not recently, and he'd take all the help he could get in finding opportunities to spend time with her. With the prices they were charging for cheesecake, he didn't think he could afford coming in during the week to purchase pastries on a regular basis.

Speaking of pastries... He lifted the lid to the cheesecake and about dropped to the floor as the sweet scent of coconut and sugar filled his lungs and weakened his knees. Golden caramel oozed down the creamy sides and dark chocolate drizzles crisscrossed the top as if guarding the rich concoction.

Nic had said that one bite would make him want to have sex, and she was wrong. Just *looking* at the dessert made him want to have sex. With her. Smeared with chocolate and caramel. Now that was an intriguing idea.

He hummed his appreciation and shot her a wink. "I don't know what I'm looking forward to most, digging into this cheesecake or our date next Friday. But I have a feeling spending time with you will be far more decadent."

She rolled her eyes, but couldn't stop the smile that lifted the corner of her mouth. "We shall see, cowboy."

"Have a good rest of the day, ladies." He scooped the box into his arms. "I know I will. And I'll see you on Friday, Miss Nicolette."

"Tell your mother hello for me, Adam," Ms. Devereux said as Nic shook her head at him in exasperation.

"Will do."

Stepping outside the little shop, the sun seemed to shine brighter and the air smelled fresher as he walked to his truck with the cake balanced in his arms. The goofy grin on his face felt as if it stretched a mile wide and for the first time in his life he felt like skipping dinner with his family to head back to the ranch and tell his friends about the pretty girl he had met.

Woman, he reminded himself. Nicolette Fournier was all woman. If he was going to keep her attention, he was going to have to step up his game. She was probably used to more sophisticated men. Men who had their own apartment or didn't come home each night wearing their work. *French men*, he thought with a sneer.

Yeah, he'd best remember to mind his manners and make her forget that she was on a date with Angus Maguire's little brother. Show her he was his own man and more than capable of treating a woman right.

As he pulled out of the shop's parking lot, the sweet scent of coconut and caramel drew his attention away from the road to the box resting on the floor of his truck. Immediately his stomach began to growl and his mouth watered. A mile down the road, his hunger didn't abate. He pulled off to the side of the road and reached down to lift the lid. The gooey dessert just lay there, supplicant, delicious-looking, begging to be tasted. What a tease.

He reached into the box and scooped up a portion with the tip of his fingers and jabbed it into his mouth before the sweet blob smeared down the front of his good shirt.

"Oh my God," he moaned as his eyes rolled back and he melted in his seat. "Oh. My. God."

She was right. He *did* want to have sex with the cheesecake. And the baker.

Holy hell. If living on the Sprawling A taught him anything, it was that a woman who loved to cook was a treasure to behold. If his date with Nic was half as good as that little bit of cheese-cake, he was going to drop to one knee and ask the girl to marry him before the night was through.

Chapter Two

N IC ROUNDED ON her aunt, who stood there, dusting her
hands off with a smile. "What the hell, Aunt Jacqui? What
were you thinking?"

"I was thinking my niece needed to get out of the house and
have a little fun. You're welcome."

"You can't go making dates for me. With a stranger, no
less."

Jacqui rolled her eyes and walked toward the kitchen. "He's
not really a stranger. The Maguires are one of Mission's original
founding families. And Adam's a sweetheart. Not to mention
pretty foxy," she added with a wink.

Foxy? Sure, the guy was cute but... Ah, who was she kidding, he was drop-dead sexy with his tight jeans riding low on his
lean hips, those broad shoulders, and devilish smile. She'd bet
her Foo Fighters concert tee with Dave Grohl's autograph that
the white highlights in his blond hair were natural and his tan
stopped at his belt buckle, although she hoped it was all over.

Growing up in cattle country, she'd seen her fair share of hot
cowboys, but there was something about Adam Maguire that
made her want to smile. And lately there were few things in the
world that gave her cause to smile.

Maybe it was his "Aww, shucks, ma'am" demeanor. That bright-eyed innocence that was usually beaten out of a person by the time they reached adulthood. Either Adam led a cushy existence free of strife, or he was one of the rare few who refused to allow anything to drag him down.

Sure, she probably could've been a little nicer to him when he first asked her out, but honestly, he surprised the hell out of her. The men in podunk Mission, Washington, regarded her as either too dark, too weird, or took too much effort to figure out. A laughable misconception, and proof of their laziness. Her needs in a partner were simple. Treat her with respect, be willing to try new things, and for the love of God, do not expect her to be the meek little woman who hung on your every word. Apparently those three things were too much to ask.

Perhaps Adam was different from the local yokels. Perhaps not. Still, it wasn't her aunt's place to make that decision for her.

"He's a stranger to me," she reminded her aunt as she followed Jacqui into the kitchen. "What if he's a closet pedophile or a Craigslist killer?"

"Please, compared to the men you've dated in the past, Adam's an Eagle Scout, altar boy, and saint all rolled into one. Again. You're welcome."

"You're nuts is what you are. Besides, you know I can't go out. There is no way I'm leaving you on your own, and you know it."

"Stop." Her aunt stopped her by covering Nic's lips with her fingers. "You have already sacrificed enough for this family. You deserve to have a little fun while you're still young enough to enjoy it. Leave the old maid thing to me. Go out. Meet people. Get laid."

Nic burst out laughing. "Aunty! I will do no such thing."

"What? Meet people or get laid? Because, honey, that man

was created to have a good time."

"Oh my God, Aunty, you are such a horn dog. Why don't you go out with him, then?"

Maybe the idea was a little ludicrous, but for a woman who was kissing fifty, her aunt was just as gorgeous as ever with her willowy frame, high cheekbones, and peachy skin. The only wrinkles on her face were around her eyes and mouth, and the streaks of gray in her long, thick hair were more recent additions.

Nic would kill to have a slender figure like her aunt, but alas, she was built more like her father's side of the family—squat, ample-bottomed, and with more curves than a bear claw. And being a baker wasn't any help to the waistline either. It was all of the tasting, with a little sample here, a tiny lick there to ensure the flavors were on point. All of those nibbles added up and spread right across her ass like jam on a cracker.

Jacqui laughed and waved her away. "Now who's being funny? And besides, the boy only had eyes for you."

Did he really?

Nope. Nope, nope, nope. Any fluttering of hope or wishful thinking needed to be shut down immediately.

She wasn't going to allow her heart to race ahead and start building any feelings for the man beyond initial attraction. There was every possibility that Adam Maguire would turn out to be just like all of the rest of the small-minded people she had grown up with. Until she had a chance to spend quality time with him, the jury was still out.

Huh. Spend quality time. In order to do so, she was going to have to go out with him.

Ya think, silly?

"Okay," she finally conceded, and ignored her inner four-teen-year-old who clapped with glee, "I'll go out with him. But I will have my phone on me the entire time, and you will call me if you need help in any way."

"You worry too much, Nic. We'll be fine for a night." Her aunt's smile turned into a mock frown as she pointed her finger in Nic's face. "And if I see you home before dawn, I'll be severely disappointed."

And that was how twisted her family was. Most people would encourage their relations to mind their manners and be demure on a first date, but not her family. They were taught to embrace the moments life had to offer. To indulge in whatever pleasures happened their way, whether it was a delicious treat, a song that moved them, even bursts of passion. The Fourniers and Devereuxes loved hard and they loved well. Not always with success, as the unknown whereabouts of Nic's father would well indicate, but they did love. And they lived.

Unfortunately, Nic only inherited part of that trait, or maybe it was her childhood that crushed her wear-her-heart-on-her-sleeve independence out of existence. It wasn't easy being the only kid wearing Doc Martens and black lipstick in the land of giant belt buckles and gingham. Every time she'd exhibited her individuality, there was someone there to tell her she was "wrong," whatever the hell that meant, which only encouraged her to throw the proverbial middle finger at the world and work that much harder at not being like the rest of her classmates.

It was only when she had left Mission and mingled with the human race was she able to distinguish what was in her heart and what was teenage angst. The need to prove how different she was ebbed and the metamorphosis of her true self took flight. Happy, confident, secure in her own skin Nicolette.

At least, that was what she had been doing until her aunt called her to come home.

Aunt Jacqui was right. She had put her life on hold since she returned. Funny how time flew when your day centered around everyone else's needs but your own.

"I would be surprised if I wasn't home before midnight," Nic said, starting to enjoy the idea of a night spent with Adam more and more. "But if he wants to kiss me, I won't turn him down."

Jacqui clapped in delight. "That's my girl."

The bell over the shop door rang at the same time a crash sounded from the living quarters of the house.

"You go," Nic said, nodding in the direction of the shop. "It's my turn anyway."

"Thanks, sweetie." Jacqui bussed her cheek with a quick kiss as she went to greet the customers.

Nic pushed open the swinging door that separated the commercial and domestic kitchens of the 1900-era two-story farmhouse from the bakery.

The home used to belong to her grandparents, and except for the addition of the bakery seven years prior, the house was mostly unchanged. The same oil paintings and family photos hung on the wall. To the right of the front door stood the giant coat rack her grandfather hung his wool coat on every night when he returned home from work. The china cabinet her great-great-grandmother brought with her when her family crossed the Oregon Trail resided in the corner of the dining room. Long gone were the original glass panels, but the dark cherry wood still gleamed in the stream of sunlight coming through the window.

This was the home she had lived in as a baby after her father skipped town on his pregnant girlfriend. Her mother had been a freshman in college and returned to the family homestead when the stress of impending motherhood and student life had become too much to bear.

Nic had loved this house as a young girl. Felt safe within its walls. And when she was eleven and her mother married the foreman of the Benedictos' farm and moved them across town, Nic returned often to spend time with her grandparents. Her mother never minded, as it allowed her more alone time with her new husband, who wasn't so keen on sharing his small home with a pre-teen.

It was in this home where she spent hours reading anything she could get her hands on. Romances, science-fiction novels, she gobbled them all up as her stereo blasted tunes by her favorite rock bands. To this day, the squeal of an electric guitar wailing away on a power solo got her hot and bothered.

The house was also the place where she had acquired an appreciation for food, learning how to bake at her grandfather's side. He had been the head pastry chef of the Mission Country Club for thirty years and was forced to retire when the arthritis in his hands got so bad, he could no longer hold a pastry bag. Two years later, he passed away. Some said it had been his diet that made his heart fail, but Nic knew it was a broken heart caused by not being able to do what he loved that did him in.

Which was why moving back to Mission sucked so hard. She *had* been doing what she loved. Living in the big city, traveling, working with some of the best chefs in the world. She had been having a ball. Sure, a steady boyfriend would have been nice during that time, but she was picky. Not only would the man of her dreams need to accept all of her, he also had to accept her choices, including her decision to not have children. The mom gene wasn't in her, and the genes she did have had no business being passed down to an innocent child.

The few men she had allowed into her personal space appeared perfectly happy with her intention to never have kids until they realized she was dead serious. Funny, it was usually the woman who rated the ability to sire offspring at the top of their list, while men preferred to enjoy the freedom that came with being childless for as long as possible. Somehow she happened to find the men who were looking for a mother for their future babies. When they realized she wasn't going to change her mind, they didn't hang around too much longer.

Mixed blessing, Nic supposed. None of her previous boyfriends would have followed her into the hell that was Mission or helped her with the only thing she was willing to sacrifice her freedom for. Mixed blessing indeed.

Another crash boomed from the reading room at the top of the stairs, and Nic raced toward the sound as two voices rose in a heated argument.

"I'm here, Mother," she shouted as she burst through the door. "I'm here."

Chapter Three

ADAM SAT IN his truck and debated for several minutes whether to climb the steps of his childhood home and go inside, or remain where he was and fill his belly with cheesecake. It was going to end up there anyway. At least this way, he'd get it all to himself.

A rap on his passenger-side window made him jump in his seat.

"What are you doing, Oops Two?" his brother Andrew asked through the window.

Oops Two. Andrew had been calling him that for as long as Adam could remember. Their brother Angus was "Oops One," since he had been an unexpected discovery during their mother's six-week checkup after Andrew's birth. Adam was a surprise from the tubal ligation that didn't take, four years after the fact. His pending arrival had prompted their father to finally go under the knife. It was either that or his mother threatened murder so she could collect the insurance money to support their growing family, or so his father claimed.

As the youngest of the heap, shit usually rolled in his direction, but that didn't mean he took it on the chin with a smile.

He lifted the pink box, drawing circles in the air with it before carefully hugging the package to his chest.

Andrew straightened. "Is that from Dulce Vita?"

With a wiggle of his brows, Adam smiled big and kissed the top of the box.

"Get out of the truck, Adam."

"Back the fuck away, Andrew."

"Get out of the truck now, or I'm coming in after you."

"If you touch me, or the box, or my truck," he added with a growl, "I'll tell Mom."

Andrew shook his head. "So mature. What are you, eight?"

Hey, being the youngest of six did have its perks. Chief among them, the unwavering protection of his mother. No matter how old he got, he'd never pass up the opportunity to evoke the power of momma bear protecting her baby cub.

Years of practice helped him dodge his brother's punch to the arm as he exited the truck with his treasure in hand. Together they climbed the front porch of the sprawling ranch house that had housed five generations of Maguires.

The home had been through many changes since its inception, especially when a new addition was built after the number of his siblings had outnumbered the available beds, but the double front door was original and bore witness to hundreds of his relatives as they left to go put their own stamp on the world.

Those who left had always been sent off with a sandwich and well wishes. Well, all except for Adam, anyway. When it had been his turn to leave the family nest, the reflection in his rearview mirror had been of his mother, dropping to her knees as she sobbed. Yeah, she had certainly pitched a fit and fell in it when he had announced he was leaving his father's operation and going to work for the Armstrongs. If he was going to stay in Mission, why not be with the rest of the family, was her argument.

Because to the rest of the family, he was still the baby with dirt caked onto the hem of his jeans, and his nose dripping as he ran and ran until he fell over exhausted trying to catch up with his big brothers. Didn't matter that he was now a grown man with a decent set of skills and expertise when it came to herding. At least with the Armstrongs, he was treated as an equal and had a space to call his own. While he loved his family dearly, there was nothing better than the freedom to sow your oats as you saw fit.

"Ma. I'm here," he called out as he entered the house and made his way to the large kitchen near the back.

"Adam?" his mother called out from over her shoulder. Her hips swung from side to side like a hula doll on a dashboard as she stirred whatever delicious-smelling concoction was in the pot. "Is that you? About time you got here. I was expecting you half an hour ago."

"I made a stop first."

Beverly Maguire turned on him with a frown and pointed at him with a wooden spoon. "I've told you a million times to call me if you're going to be late."

He dodged the gravy-covered spoon and dropped a kiss to her cheek. "I'm not late. I told you I'd be here after work. It's after work. Where is everybody?"

"What am I? Furniture?" His sister-in-law Ginny said from the sink where she was rinsing off lettuce.

"If you were furniture," he replied, "you'd be a lovely china cabinet. Sturdy and filled with nice things."

"You are so lucky I'm not holding a knife right now," she said with a shake of her head. Her dark-blonde ponytail swung back and forth as she returned to her task.

"Your father and brothers are coming in and washing up," his mother said. Her eyes lit up when she noticed the pink box in his hands. "Ooo…what's that?"

"Something sweet for the sweetest woman in the world."

"Oh my God." Ginny gagged and rolled her eyes.

"Oh, my favorite," his mother exclaimed as she peeked inside the box. "But why is there a hunk missing?"

"Andrew tackled me when I got here and took a swipe."

"That boy," she said, then nodded at the refrigerator. "Go ahead and make room. Move whatever you have to."

In typical Maguire fashion, the refrigerator was about full to bursting, with two cakes and a chocolate cream pie waiting to be devoured. It took some reshuffling, but he was able to store all of the desserts away safely and turned just in time to see his mother thwack Andrew in the back of the head as he took his turn at the sink to wash his hands.

"Ow, Ma!" he shouted. "What was that for?"

"You know why. Stop doing it."

Adam sucked in a laugh lest he give himself away, and made his way into the family room where his three nephews were camped out in front of the television, staring diligently at the video game flashing on the screen. "Hey, fellas."

"Uncle Adam," they shouted, and the youngest, Spencer, jumped up from his seat and ran to his side.

"Thank goodness you're here." Spencer pointed to his brother and cousin. "I need you to teach them a lesson. They're being jerks and won't let me have a turn. Just because they're going into middle school in the fall, they think their shit don't stink."

"Whoa." Adam clapped his hand over the ten-year-old's mouth. "You kiss your momma with that mouth, boy? She'd kick your ass if she heard you cussing."

"They just get me so mad," he replied and his eyes boggled with frustration and a tinge of pink washed over his chubby cheeks. "Besides, I hear Daddy and the uncles swear all of the time."

"Yeah, well, that's because they're adults. When you've registered to vote and pay taxes, you're allowed to swear all you want. Until then, keep it clean, kid."

"I'll try."

"Believe me, Spence, I feel your frustration. Come on, let's show 'em how it's done." He sat on the floor next to his nephews. "Okay, guys, let's play four-player, and Spencer is on my team."

"What?" the older boys grumbled until Adam started clucking like a chicken.

"Okay, dude," Jacob said. "We'll take you. And the baby, too."

Before Spencer popped off with another curse word over being called a baby by a kid only two years older than him, Adam sent him a wink and handed him a controller.

Ten minutes later, he and Spencer high-fived as they won the third round in a row.

"Ah-ha!" Spencer crowed. "Take that, suckas."

"Zach," Adam said to his older brother, who stood watching them at the entrance to the room. "I think your boys have issues. What are you teaching them at home?"

"I blame our parents," he replied with a shrug. "I think sibling rivalry is hereditary."

Their mother appeared behind her son's shoulder. "Supper's on. Come and get it, boys."

A herd of stampeding cattle made less noise than they did as the clan gathered around the dinner table and took their seats.

The younger boys had their own table in the corner of the room while the adults took their places at the table where they had sat since they themselves were kids. Oh, there had been a few changes here and there as wives came and went. Zach's wife, Ginny, sat by her husband across the table from Adam, who sat near the end of the table near his mother. Since Travis's divorce a few years ago, the space his wife had sat was now occupied by Zach's little girl and her high chair.

Adam often wondered what would happen when any more of his brothers got married. As it was, they were so cramped around the table, he could cut his and his mother's food with one pass of the knife.

And with that thought, an image of Nic came to mind, sitting by his side at the family table. They'd have to be seated so close, he'd be able to feel the heat of her thigh against his where they touched. She'd probably be horrified by his father and his good ol' boy philosophies, but if anyone could verbally spar with the old man and hold her own, he'd bet his money on Nic.

Funny. He hadn't thought about bringing a girl home for a long time. Angela had been his last girlfriend, but that had ended months ago. And the last time he had brought her to a family dinner was early on in their year-long relationship. She had refused to eat anything that wasn't organic or if it came from a cow. Since his father owned the largest cattle ranch in Central Washington, and she was dating a cowboy, her aversion to beef was viewed by his family as a fatal flaw. The jokes and zingers lobbed at her by his brothers had gotten so bad, she had left in tears.

That should have been a clue to end things with her back then, but she was so beautiful with her long strawberry-blonde hair and killer bod, he had been willing to overlook her bias against the family business in exchange for sex, shallow as that seemed. It was when he realized Angela was pulling him further away from the people and things he loved that he finally drove the final nail in that coffin.

Something of his thoughts must have shown on his face for his mother patted him on the hand before she cleared her throat and addressed the family. "Let us pray."

They all clasped their hands and bowed their heads as Beverly led the family prayer.

"Dear Heavenly Father, we thank you for another day on this glorious planet, and the joys you have bestowed upon us. We are grateful to feel your embrace as we gather in the bosom"—the younger boys' quiet snickers made Adam smile— "of family on the anniversary of my beloved Scott's birth. We ask you to watch over us, and show us the strength and courage to face the obstacles that have yet to come our way. If my precious boy is with you, I know he too is watching over us with the love and patience that was the most beautiful part of his nature. But if he is lost in this world, tell him that his family loves and misses him and wants him to come home. In Jesus's name, amen."

"Amen," they all murmured, and Adam's gaze wandered to the empty seat at the table where his brother Scott used to sit.

It had been three years ago, on an icy winter day much like all the others, when several Marines dressed in their fancy suits appeared at the door of the Maguire house and informed them that his brother and his entire Elite Recon unit had gone MIA in the Baltic Sea. All were presumed dead.

That was the first and only time Adam had seen his father go stone cold and became barely able to function. The old man couldn't speak more than a word or two at a time for days. His only companion during that time had been his horse as he roamed the vast property line from sunup to beyond sundown. Funeral arrangements had fallen to Travis and the older brothers, as their mother hadn't been in much better shape to take on the task.

All they had to bury was an American flag. And because of the nature of Scott's job with the Marines, Beverly was convinced her son was still alive. Three years later and they hadn't heard a thing, but Beverly continued to hope and made sure there was a place setting at the dinner table every night. Even as the number of family members grew, there was always a place for Scott.

"So, how is Jacqui doing over at the bakeshop?" his mother asked.

"Ms. Devereux is doing fine," he replied as he heaped two spoonsful of mashed potatoes on his plate. "Says hello, by the way. You know, it's been years since I've been there myself. I forgot how good it smells."

"There is nothing like the scent of fresh-baked bread." Beverly smiled. "If I'd known you were stopping by there, I'd have asked you to bring some rolls."

"Maybe next time. Actually, I have a date with her niece, Nic, next Friday."

Across the table, Angus sputtered around a mouthful of food. "Nicolette? *You* have a date with Nicolette?"

Adam froze with his fork mid-air. There was something about the way Angus pronounced Nic's full name that made his hackles rise. "Yeah. What about it?"

"I, um, I just didn't think she was your type, was all," he replied with a shrug, but there was a wariness in his eyes Adam took to mean his brother questioned his intelligence.

"She's beautiful, smart, and can cook. She's my type."

"She's also weird," Angus' wife, Emily, added. "I remember in school she was always wearing black clothes and dark makeup. And those big clunky boots, remember, Ginny?"

Ginny nodded. "And she'd never talk to anyone, just stare at you from the corner of the room. And she never attended any of the social functions. And still doesn't, if you noticed."

"Did anyone ever go up to her and say hello? Or invite her personally?" he asked, not liking the snotty tones of his sisters-in-law.

"Of course not," Emily answered with a toss of her dark hair. "If she wanted to hang, she had to ask."

"I don't know," he said. "If either of you were in my grade, I probably wouldn't have said boo to you either."

Ginny snorted. "Come on, Adam. I know it's been a while since high school, but you remember how it was. You were either part of the crowd or you weren't."

Unfortunately, she had a point.

No matter the generation, there were always the same cliques in school. You had the rich kids, the poor kids, the jocks, the brainiacs, and the outcasts. And in Mission you also had the group of kids who didn't fit in anywhere because their sole function was to work the family business and only attended school because it was the law. Most of the time, those kids were homeschooled anyway.

Adam liked to think he was one of those people who made friends with everyone. But if he stopped and really thought about it, his closest friends had either been on the football team or hung out at all of the games. Since practically the entire town supported the high school football program, he had assumed that meant he was friends with everyone.

"Nic is a lovely girl," his mother said and patted him on the back of his hand. "Very talented. I'm sure you'll have a good time. How is her momma doing?"

The question caught him off guard. "I don't know. We didn't discuss her." Was there something about Nic's mother he should know about?

Before he had the chance to ask, his father cut in. "Any

more of your co-workers planning on engaging in any illicit affairs? I had a nice little bump in business after George's daughter shacked up with your friends."

"That was such horseshit."

"Adam!" his mother said as his sisters-in-law gasped. "Language."

"Well, it was. And still is. It's nobody's business what those three do in the privacy of their own home."

"That's just it," Travis said. "They had to take it out in broad daylight."

"They did not," Adam shot back. "Ben and Colby are two of the classiest guys I know. And I'm glad to call them friends. I think it's great they found someone to make them happy. Is it strange? Maybe. But it's real, and more honest than any relationship I've ever been in."

Zach squinted at him from over his drinking glass. "How much daytime television are you watching? I think you need to cut back, Dr. Phil."

"Ah, never mind." Why waste the energy in trying to get them to see it like he did?

Aside from Scott's death, in the grand scheme in life, the Maguires had had it pretty good. Sure, they'd hit a rough patch now and again, but never did they have to endure true, soul-shaking hardships like those who worked at the Sprawling A had.

It was about six months after little Luke Armstrong died that he joined the A. Watching the pain Greta and Trey suffered through had taken its toll on everyone, but by some miracle, they recovered. The shit Gabriella had to put up with her ex-husband kidnapping her was another nightmare, and then there was the circus that pulled into town when Ben and Colby took Faith in as their mutual girl. Holy hell, you'd have thought the world was coming to an end the way some of the townsfolk went on. The scandal cost Trey some business with the local groceries for a little while, and access to some of their suppliers.

Yeah, at times it felt as if they were on an episode of some crazy reality show, but through it all, the ranch persevered. With each obstacle, the Armstrongs and their friends grew closer together, and Adam was proud to be considered one of their clan.

If only his blood family were as tight as his family on the A.

Sitting there in the crowded dining room, Adam had never felt more alone. It was as if he were an exhibit at a zoo and his family was just passing by.

These were his relations, yet they didn't know him. Like, *know* him know him, like his friends did. On one end of the table, his father was talking Maguire business with his brothers, and on his end his mother was asking Ginny about her latest DIY craft project. Not only did his brothers work on the ranch, they had all built homes on the ranch too. There was even a plot of land staked out for him, but he loved sharing the house with Jack and Rafe at the A.

Again, his eyes wandered to the place setting for Scott. Was that why his big brother had left the ranch? If there was ever an oddball in the Maguire clan, it was Scott. Tall, thin, and the only child to inherit their mother's dark hair, he was the artist in the family, and had preferred spending his time drawing comic books and playing video games than working with the livestock. Oh, he pulled his share and did his chores, but ranching was never in his blood.

It about killed their mother when he followed his friends off to college in Texas. And when he joined the Marines, well, that bit of news nearly sent them all into shock. The decision had come from so out of the blue, it could have been a headline on the *Weekly World News* and been just as believable.

But Scott had thrived in the military, and the last time Adam had seen him, Scott had turned into a big, brawny badass. Even Zach and Travis were afraid to pull any of their old slapstick routines on their "little" brother.

It was seeing his brother's transformation that had given Adam the courage to leave the family business. To strive for an identity that wasn't tied to the Maguire name. He might not have been as brave as his brother, or Nic Fournier, who sought her freedom in another country, but at least he made some effort. That had to count for something in the grand scheme of life, right?

For the rest of the evening, Adam held his tongue and nodded with a polite smile when required. When the clock finally struck an hour that was reasonable for him to make his exit and he had had his fill of cheesecake, he stifled a relieved sigh and prepared to say his good-byes.

He hugged the kids, gave fist pumps to the older boys, and nodded at his father across the room. That was about all of the sentimentality his father was comfortable with. As was usual, his mother followed him onto the porch and pressed a container of leftovers in his hands.

"You got awfully quiet in there, sweet pea. Did your father upset you with his comments about your friends?"

He winced at the nickname his mother had called him since his birth. "Kinda. I know their relationship sounds weird. *They* know it sounds weird. But they're so happy. When I look at them, I can't imagine them apart. It's nice. And I—" *I'm jealous as hell.* "I hope to be as lucky in finding my match."

"Oh, you will, sweetie." She clasped the sides of his face between her palms. "You have a lot to offer a girl. And you'd have even more if you moved back home and built the house on the lot that's waiting for you."

"Ah, Ma. We've been over this before."

"I know. But I am hopeful that you'll change your mind and return to where you belong. Here. With your family."

"The Armstrongs and everyone at the ranch are my family, too."

"No," she said in a firm tone. "They are your friends. *We* are your family." Her eyes got wide and began to shimmer in the glow of the porch light. "Why are you so determined to be away from us? Didn't we love you enough? Can't you feel our love?"

There it was. The big, sad, eyes with tears clinging to her lashes as she lamented his need for independence. Usually the guilt train departed earlier in the evening, but it was a rare occasion when he avoided the journey altogether.

"I feel your love, Ma. At times I'm smothered in it. But you know how I like to be on my own. And I'm only across town. It's not like I—" He almost said *joined the military*, but that little nugget would ruffle her mama bird feathers even more and bring out the claws to sink into him in an effort to keep him close. "It's not like I don't visit often."

"I just want my babies close to the nest. Is that so wrong?" she said with a sniff.

"Nope. Just like my need to have some space isn't wrong either." He dropped a kiss to her cheek. "Good night, Ma. Love ya."

"Call me or text me when you get home," she hollered after him.

Yeah, yeah. He waved from his truck and drove down the lane. With each quarter mile that passed, he felt the weight of family expectations fall away. The stench of cows faded, replaced with the sweet scent of apples as he passed miles of farmland.

As a cluster of lights appeared in the distance, the acrid odor of manure grew strong again as he drove onto Armstrong land and the Sprawling A ranch. The crunch of gravel under his tires was a welcoming chime as he turned onto the lane and drove past the main house. Greta and Trey waved at him from the front porch swing as they rocked back and forth, cuddled in each other's arms. Or mostly cuddled as Greta's pregnant belly kept her from hugging everybody as tightly as she once did.

The house he shared with Jack and Rafe was down a ways beyond the horse barn and breeding area. A black Ford 150 and a beat-up '88 Chevy that was more rust than paint were parked in front.

As soon as Adam stepped across the threshold, the fellas were on him, immediately holding out their hands for the leftovers in his grip.

"What was it tonight?" Jack asked as he lifted the lid on the container.

"Pot roast," he answered.

"Excellent. Greta made pork chops. I like it when it's something different." He crossed to the open kitchen and retrieved two forks, handing one to Rafe as he returned to his seat on the couch that had seen better days. Even though they had probably just arrived from dinner with the Armstrongs, Jack and Rafe were always hungry for Beverly Maguire's leftovers.

"How's the *familia*?" Rafe asked, gravy dripping down his chin.

"Good. Same old, same old. Hey! I thought you were going to wait to watch the game until I got back."

"We barely started it. Nothing happened first quarter, anyway." Jack's response was interrupted with a loud belch that set Rafe off with a belch in return.

The two erupted into laughter, and a belching and name-calling contest that brought into question the purity of their mothers' virtue ensued while Adam sat back in his chair with a huge grin and soaked it all in.

Yep. It was good to be home.

Chapter Four

"'B YE, AUNT JACQUI,"** Nic called out the moment she spotted Adam's truck pull up to the front of the house.

"Nic, wait—"

Yeah, no.

Before her aunt could stop her, she was out the door and down the stairs. If given the chance, Jacqui would not hesitate to invite Adam in and talk for a spell. A first date was not the time to expose a man to the inner sanctum of one's personal crazytown.

Adam was climbing out of the truck as she approached. "You didn't have to rush out, I could have...uh. I, uh..." He trailed off as his jaw dropped and he stared at her with wide, blinking eyes.

"What?" She looked down at her shirt then did a quick pirouette to try to see her backside. Had she spilled something down her front, or have floured handprints on her person? "Is there something wrong?"

"What?" He shook his head as if waking from a dream. "No. It's, uh, just..." He floundered a bit with a few stops and starts before he sighed. "Shoot, Nic. I gotta be honest. You look hot.

Smoking hot." He held up his hands with his fingers forming a frame. "I mean, your rack looks amazing, which I know makes me sound like a big ol' perv, and you'll call the date off right now. But I don't think I'll be able to look away from your boobs. They are *awesome*."

Wow. An actual candid, honest response. How novel. And completely charming.

After work, she had done the girly thing and changed her clothes four times before settling on her favorite black blouse with the low-cut sweetheart neckline, and red jeans. The outfit was comfortable, flirty, and made her feel sexy. Confident without walking around with a chip on her shoulder and daring anyone to make a smartass comment. When all was said and done, it didn't matter what anyone else thought about her clothes as long as she was happy, but she was glad Adam enjoyed her efforts.

She pushed her hands into her back pockets, a move that thrust her chest out further, and she chuckled. "Well, that's a first. Thank you for your honesty."

Adam blinked with surprise. "You don't think I'm a Neanderthal who needs to remember boobs are not just sexual objects?"

God, he was hysterical. "I think you're a man who enjoys women. And don't stress too much. If I didn't want you to look at my boobs, I would have worn a turtleneck."

"Nope." He shook his head. "Wouldn't have helped. With you covered up, all I'd be thinking about is what your cleavage looked like. This is much better."

Adam continued to eat her up with a hungry gaze, so she returned the favor. He was so handsome in his blue and white checked shirt and tight jeans, especially with the sleeves rolled up to his elbows and a few of the silver snaps open down the front to reveal a golden chest. His shaved cheeks appeared so smooth, she wanted to plant a big kiss on the skin just to see if she'd leave a perfect red lip print. Actually, she wanted to leave lip prints all over his lean body.

Darn Aunt Jacqui and her illicit suggestions. All week long, she hadn't been able to think about anything else but stripping Adam Maguire naked and getting him dirty.

"So…" she said after several more seconds of staring at him as if he were a creamy dessert in a display case. "Where to?"

"Oh! Yeah. Sorry." He ran to the other side of the truck and opened the passenger door. "Your chariot, my dear."

"Thank you."

She settled in her seat and took note of the clean interior and the brand-new, apple-shaped air freshener hanging from the rearview mirror. The cinnamon and fruit scent tickled her nose and was a little overwhelming in the small confines of the truck, but she appreciated the effort.

Adam jumped behind the wheel and flashed her a smile before starting off down the road. "I thought we'd go to The Crescent. There's going to be a cover band playing tonight."

"The Crescent. Great," she said, and tried to keep her smile in place. "Are we going to be meeting your friends there?"

"Maybe. I didn't make any plans with them. This night is all about spending time with you." He winked. "But I'm sure we'll run into someone I know."

She nodded with the same plastic smile on her lips and willed her racing heart to slow.

The Crescent Moon Bar. The hub of local nightlife, and the place to go to "be seen" and have a wild time. Many a scandal had been made at The Crescent, which was why all of the cool kids did whatever it took to get inside before they became of age. Then those cool kids grew up to be snobby adults who returned in a sad attempt to relive their glory years.

Only once had she been inside the honky-tonk, and that was on her eighteenth birthday when her best friend Megan had gifted her with a fake ID. The two of them had walked right in and ordered a round of beers without any incident.

Megan was a kindred spirit, who shared her love of the arts, Nine Inch Nails, and a hatred of all things country. The day after they graduated, they loaded up Megan's '93 Honda Accord and left a good line of tire tread on the road as they had shot out of town and headed for the city.

But on that night, her friend had gotten it into her head that she was going to lose her virginity and had chosen a handsome farmhand to do the deed. Unfortunately, his girlfriend wasn't too keen on the idea, and when she caught them getting hot and heavy in a dark corner of the dance floor, fists flew and hair was pulled.

Of course, being the good friend that she was, Nic had jumped into the fray, short lived as it was. One would have thought you learned how to fight when living on a farm, but apparently that wasn't true. All Nic had to do was dodge the girlfriend's fist, latch on to her arm, bend it behind her back, and wait it out until the police arrived. Not her proudest moment, but it did solidify her status as a badass.

"How long did you live in Paris?"

"Huh?" She shook her head from the past. "Oh, just over a year."

"And you miss it?"

"Terribly. I miss all of Europe. Edinburgh was a blast. London, lovely. Berlin, well, I may have gotten married in Berlin. Still not sure about that. But I love to visit local places, too. New Orleans, Manhattan, Nashville."

"Sweetness, those aren't local." He shook his head with a

low whistle. "Golly, you get around."

"Well, what about you?" she asked. "Where's your favorite place to travel?"

"Me? Oh. Well, when I was a kid, we'd go camping at the Pot Holes and Chelan once a year. But that's about it."

"You've never been out of the state?" Surprising, but not completely implausible. Especially considering the way small-town people tended to keep in their lane. "What about to the city?"

"Nope. Never been."

Okay, now she was totally shocked. "Are you serious? Never once? Wait, didn't you go to Vegas for Mark's wedding? When Greta ordered Trey's birthday cake, she was talking about how everyone on the ranch was going."

"Ben and I stayed behind to keep an eye on the cows. Anyway, I don't like to fly."

"You don't like to fly, or don't like airplanes? There is a difference."

"Airplanes." He shuddered as if someone walked on his grave. "They're cramped, tiny, and kept up by only manmade engineering and the grace of God. I'm good with keeping my feet on the ground."

"I'd say I felt sorry for you, but you don't look like you're the least bit upset about missing out on exploring the world."

He flashed her a big grin and shrugged. "That's 'cause I'm not. Everything I care about is right here in Mission."

Pity and jealousy left a bitter taste in her mouth. To miss out on witnessing the beauty in the world was, in her opinion, a great tragedy. The sounds, the smells, the people. A magical tapestry of colors and experiences that added a richness to life that was immeasurable.

But if Adam was happy with life as he had it, then who was

she to judge? It must be nice to have found life's joys right in your own backyard. He was either really lucky or incredibly naïve. A little bit of both was her guess.

"Whoa," Adam exclaimed as he turned in to the parking lot of The Crescent. "It's packed."

Oh, goody.

He found a parking space in the far corner of the lot and came to a stop. As she reached for the door handle, he tsked and waved his hands at her. He jumped out of the truck and ran to her side, opening the door with a flourish. After she climbed out, he shut the door and presented his arm.

"You have nice manners there, cowboy," she drawled and wrapped her hands around his biceps. Ooo…and nice guns, too.

"My momma would smack me upside the head if I didn't. Shall we, Miss Fournier?"

Having a handsome cowboy on her arm was quite the confidence boost, and the swagger rocking her hips as he escorted her inside was not to be helped.

"Huh, what do you know," she murmured once her eyes adjusted to the low light. "Same old, same old."

Yep, The Crescent Moon Bar hadn't changed much in the ten years since she'd been there. The hardwood floors were still covered with a fine layer of top soil and hay, the amber lighting was dim enough to make everyone look prettier than they actually were, and the mirror behind the bar had the same long crack across the corner from the time Gloria, who owned the Cut N' Curl, found her first husband getting cozy with another woman and threw her shoe at his head and missed. At least, that was the story Nic had heard as a child. Since the woman whom Mr. Cut N' Curl was canoodling with was Gloria's sister, it had caused quite a scandal.

The scent of beer, dirt, and fried food floated in the air in hazy clouds. Thank goodness she had chosen clothes that were machine washable.

On either side of the stage were two large cages that were empty at the moment, and instead of a DJ spinning tracks, a band was front and center, jamming to a country song Nic had never heard before. Of course, since she didn't listen to country music, every song was new to her.

"Holy shit," a man exclaimed as they passed the bar. "If it isn't Nicolette Fournier."

Behind the counter, a tall, dark-haired man stared at her in open-mouthed surprise. Heat hit her cheeks as a decade-old embarrassment tickled her belly. With a lift of her chin, she swallowed the roiling sensation and smiled. "Hello, Mike. It's been a while."

"A while, my ass." He tossed a bar towel over his broad shoulder and placed both hands on the bar. "I thought you vowed never to step foot in here again."

"Let's just say I'm turning over a new leaf."

"Is there something I need to know?" Adam asked.

Mike chuckled. "My first week on the job here as a bouncer, Nic and her friend Megan snuck in with fake IDs and tore the house down."

"He's exaggerating," she interjected. "And it was all Megan's fault."

He gestured with a beefy hand. "Those three red tables and the set of chairs in that corner were purchased to replace the ones they broke."

"Again, it wasn't me. It was Stephanie Dodson who got pissed that her boyfriend Ryan had his hand down Megan's pants. I was just trying to keep people from getting maimed."

Mike's smile widened and she couldn't stop the flutter of awareness of his masculine charm. Man, he had always been a good-looking guy. The classic bad-boy type in denim and shit-kickers. He had been Megan's first choice to take her virginity, but he had shot that down right quick. "You still keep in touch with Megan?"

"Yep. She lives in New York. She's a lawyer now. Married to a dentist and expecting her second child."

"Good for her. You know, it *is* good to see you, Nic."

"Thanks." The blast of sincerity in his dark eyes was unexpected, and she wasn't sure what to do with it. Kind of like when someone got you a Christmas gift and you had nothing to give in return. She shifted her weight and searched for something intelligent to say. "And look at you. You're now the bartender."

Yeah. Real intelligent there, Captain Obvious.

"Oh, it's sadder than that," he said and came around to join them. "I own the place now. Follow me. I've been saving your table."

"Do you want to stay?" Adam asked her. "I didn't know you had a past here."

A past. She snorted. The way he said it made her sound infamous.

"A person without a past is a person who hasn't lived, I say." She patted him on his chest and was momentarily distracted by the hard muscles of his pectorals. "We can stay. That was a long time ago, and I'm sure Stephanie Dodson is living somewhere in the city with a doctor for a husband."

Mike chuckled. "She married a doctor, all right. Didn't you know? She lives in Ellensburg and is married to Doc Lawson."

"No, I didn't. Then again, I don't mingle much with the locals. I didn't know Doc Lawson had a son who was also a doctor."

"He doesn't," Adam replied, sharing Mike's laughter. "She married Doc Lawson himself. As in *old man* Doc Lawson."

"No shit," she exclaimed. He had to be at least twenty-five years older than his wife. "Isn't that something. Well, even if I were to run into her, I can be civil. Lead the way, good sir."

As Adam escorted her through the bar, he waved and smiled at the people they passed. In return, they received smiles that turned into confused frowns the moment they realized it was her on his arm. Under the screaming guitar solo from the band, she heard murmurs of their conversations.

"Who is that?"

"Is that the girl from the bakery?"

"I thought she was part vampire and had to wait for the sun to go down."

Now that comment did make her chuckle, and she added a little extra shimmy to her stride as she walked beside Adam. People were too up into everyone's business in this town. Heaven forbid she be a private person and keep to herself. Besides, a little sense of mystery was good for the image.

Mike took their drink order as Adam pulled out her chair, and she settled into her seat at the tall cocktail table.

"I can't help but wonder what you had to do to actually reserve a table on a busy night like this."

"I have friends who have friends," he said with a shrug. "And I wanted you to enjoy the music in comfort. I know I'm not fancy or sophisticated, but I can most certainly make an effort to provide you a little of what you're used to."

"Are you for real?" she burst out. "Sorry. Sorry. That didn't sound right. It's just..." she sighed. If he only knew about some of the lowlifes she had dated in an attempt to be edgy or walk on the wild side. In comparison, Adam was a choir boy, a knight in shining armor, and the billionaire playboy. "Thank you for the consideration. I'm not used to, well, I'm not used to...that. If you are genuine, I will respond. Right now, I'm responding. A lot."

"Does that mean you like me?"

It meant she wanted to crawl onto his lap, feel his arms wrap tight around her, and inhale his scent. "I've always liked you. Now I like you more."

His smile was blinding in the dimly lit room. He reached for the base of her seat and pulled her toward him until their thighs touched and her shoulder fit under his arm. "That's good. I like you more, too."

The waitress dropped their beers on the table, and Adam lifted his for a toast. "So tell me all about Nic Fournier."

"Ha, ha," she said. "You first."

"I was born a poor black child," he began.

"You're familiar with *The Jerk*?" she sputtered in surprise.

"Oh yeah. My mom is a big Steve Martin fan. When I was seven, I had the flu and was home sick. She put the movie on while she was mending the holes in our shirts. Us boys tended to be tough on our clothes. Man, I laughed so hard, I almost coughed up a lung. That movie is hysterical. Anyway..."

Adam then launched into another story about his mom and his brothers. She in turn talked about being an only child, which boggled his mind.

Conversation flowed between them in an endless babble as they talked. Just talked. About their day, their tastes in music, current town events. They talked about everything and nothing, and it was fabulous.

She liked the way his eyes lit up as he told her stories about his friends on the ranch, and she especially liked his laugh as he regaled her with the tale of the latest prank he had pulled on his roommates Jack and Rafe. She liked the look of his hand as he gripped the beer bottle, and the way his throat worked as he swallowed. She also liked the way his gaze would travel to her cleavage when he thought she wasn't noticing, then pop back up. But most of all, she loved it when the music grew too loud and he'd lean in close to speak in her ear and his breath brushed her cheek. The citrus spice scent of his aftershave was heavenly, and the brim of his cowboy hat blocked her vision to create an intimate space for just the two of them. Well, as intimate as a couple could be in the middle of a crowded bar, anyway.

If she had been told that she'd be in The Crescent, listening to a honky-tonk cover band, with a handsome young cowboy gazing at her as if she were a decadent chocolate, all while having a good time, she would have asked them the name of their drug dealer.

But there she was, having a grand time. Hell, she was having a great time. Okay, score one for Aunt Jacqui. She'd have to make sure to take over her aunt's chores for the week in thanks for making her accept Adam's date. Would she say those words to her aunt out loud? Hell, no. But she'd still show her appreciation.

The band launched into a grand finale of "Free Bird," which brought Adam to his feet with a woot and a holler. Several cellphones were raised in the air with flashlight apps on, and Adam joined them, swaying back and forth in time with the music. Melodic swaying turned into raucous jumping as the guitar solo kicked into high gear, rising to a crescendo. When the last notes stopped vibrating in her ear, Adam grabbed her hand.

"How's about a dance?"

"I'd love to."

"Then come with me, darlin'."

Nic proceeded him to the dance floor and started to rock out to the rolling beat of a classic Bon Jovi song.

Oh, how she loved dancing. Losing herself in the rhythm of a song and the crush of bodies all moving as one. While riding the musical waves, she didn't have to think about life and her place therein, just move where her body took her, and let go.

But dancing was always better when you had a partner. She turned to look for Adam, then froze, stupefied by the scene before her.

There was a phrase she'd seen a thousand times, usually embroidered on a pillow or wall hanging, and one of the lines was "Dance as if no one is watching." Apparently Adam took that message to heart, except she was watching and wondering if the man was for real or if this was one of his pranks.

He had tucked his hands under his armpits and was bobbing up and down like a chicken looking for a juicy worm. His lips were pinched tight and his head wobbled on his neck as if it were made out of Silly Putty.

"Whoa. White man dancing," she muttered to herself. "Adam. What'cha doing?"

"I'm getting my groove on," he replied and did a stutter step to the left.

"Really?"

"Of course. I take my jams seriously."

She glanced to the right and left, and when she caught the eye of a nearby couple, they just nodded and went back to their dancing.

"I can't believe I'm going to say this. Can you stop. Please? The Latina in me is about to cry."

He pulled up short. "What's wrong?"

"Has anyone ever taught you how to dance?"

"Not formally."

"Okay. Look, I am usually the last person to tell anyone how to enjoy their music, but let me teach you a move or two. Please. And if you don't like it, you can go back to the chicken-man dance."

"You seriously don't like my dancing?" He looked like a little boy who had a favorite video game taken away. He was so crestfallen, she was ready to allow him to revert to his haphazard ways.

"It's great. I just fear for my safety. Don't want to catch an elbow to the eye or anything."

A dimple formed in his cheek with his lopsided smile. "Okay, dancing queen. Show me what you got."

"All right, this move is called finding the beat. Feet slightly apart. Stand up straight. Now, feel the rhythm pulse through you and bounce your knees in time to the beat." She bit back a giggle as he began to resemble a bobble head doll. "Slow it down a little. There we go. Now we're going to go back and forth. Step touch, step touch, step touch, step touch." She reached for his hands and placed them on her hips. "Like this."

He pulled her into the curve of his body. "Hey. This is nice."

More than nice, she thought as her lumps and bumps filled in the dips and valleys of his muscled torso. If she leaned forward, she'd be able to rest her ear right over his heart, but she resisted the pull. Besides, she loved looking up into his eyes and that adorable smile as they rocked back and forth.

"Ready to get a little crazy?" she asked.

"Always."

"Take a small, diagonal step forward, then one back. That's right. Nice and easy."

Adam's smile widened as he guided them into a circle and his hands slipped over her hips and around her backside. Her hands weren't idle either, as she ran her palms over his chest and the cap of his shoulders. His thigh slipped between hers, and when he tipped his head, the brim of his hat again created that cozy, intimate environment that made her feel as if she were the only girl in the world.

"You are so amazingly beautiful," he murmured, drawing her closer until her breasts crushed against his chest.

His breath swept over her lips that parted in anticipation of his kiss.

"Adam Maguire. Is that you?"

They jumped apart as Adam was slapped on the back by a beefy hand attached to an even beefier cowboy standing behind him.

"Hey, Jonas," Adam greeted the newcomer with a hardy handshake. "Long time no see, bro."

"Yeah, haven't seen you much since you broke up with my sister. Kinda understandable."

A strawberry-blond pixie of a girl hip-checked Nic and wrapped her arms around Adam's waist. "Adam, I've missed you."

"Hey, Angela," he said with a grimace and tried to extricate himself out of her hold without having much luck. His movements reminded Nic of a cat trying shake an extra-sticky piece of tape off its paw.

"I've been thinking a lot about what you said about us not having the same plans for the future, but you're wrong. I want exactly what you want. Home. Family. What do you say? I want you back. And once we're together, everything will be great again."

Want you back?

Holy hell. Nic winced as if she took an empty beer can to the forehead. Of course Adam had dated little miss prom queen. It was just her luck that the one guy in Mission she found interesting in the romantic sense had once dated one of the banes of her high school experience.

"Angela, I broke up with you because things *weren't* great." He stepped around his former girlfriend and took Nic by the hand. "I've moved on."

"Wait. What? With *her*?" Angela's eyes boggled. "The princess of darkness? You have got to be kidding. I thought you were just being nice and it was a pity dance."

"The only thing deserving pity right now is you," Adam said as he started to turn back to Nic.

"Don't turn your back on me," she shrieked, then looked around the room with a furtive glance as she must have realized she sounded like a shrew. "What I mean is I'm not done talking to you. Adam, we were made for each other. Don't you see? I complete you."

Whoa. If the poor girl didn't appear so heartbroken and delusional, Nic would have burst out laughing at such an arrogant statement.

Apparently Adam appeared to feel the same way as Nic, because he shook his head and looked past the indignant woman to her brother. "Jonas, you better get your sister out of here before she makes a fool out of herself."

Angela gasped in outrage and actually stomped her foot, which finally sent Nic into giggles. If steam really could come out of someone's ears, thick clouds would've been rolling from Angela's as she flushed bright red.

"You want to see a fool? I'll show you a fool." Angela reached out and grabbed Nic under the arm in the sensitive part of her triceps and dragged her across the floor toward the DJ. "Hey, Julio. I have your next cage girl right here."

"Get your hands off me," Nic growled and wrenched her arm away. "What is wrong with you?"

Angela invaded her personal space until Nic choked on a cloud of flowery, cheap drugstore perfume.

"If you think I'm gonna let you worm your way into Adam's life just so you can get your hands on some Maguire money, you have another thing coming," she said with a curl to her lip.

"Wow." Nic stood there and blinked for a while as she waited for the world to right itself. "That is about the stupidest thing I've ever heard you say, Angela. And I've heard you say a lot of stupid shit. Are you projecting much? A little bitter he broke up with you?"

"I don't know what has gotten into him lately, but he'll snap out of this weird phase he's been in of wanting to try new things. He'll remember who his friends are and who he is. And then he'll come crawling back to me."

"I wouldn't hold my breath, sweetheart. Adam is an adult who seems pretty confident about what he wants, and it ain't you."

"Nic," Adam said as he caught up to them. "Are you all right?"

"I'm fine. It appears that princess sunshine here thinks you two have unfinished business."

"Damn it, Angela," he spat. "What are you trying to prove?"

From over their heads, the DJ's voice bellowed over the loudspeaker. "We have a fresh face joining us in the cage tonight. What's your name, darlin'?" he asked, leaning over his station and looking at Nic.

"Nicolette," Angela shouted. "Her name is Nicolette."

"All right. Let's give le femme Nicolette a hand, folks."

Wait. What?

Everyone in the bar was looking their way, whistling and clapping their hands as the DJ opened the door of the cage that took up the front corner of the stage.

"You want me to go in there?" she asked. "And do what?"

"Shake that fat ass of yours," Angela answered. "Or are you too scared?"

Ah-ha. So that was Angela's game. Embarrass Nic in front of

Adam and most of the town, and shame her into never showing her face in public again.

Nic wasn't sure what was more juvenile—the challenge itself, or the acceptance of such a challenge.

Adam stopped her with a hand on her shoulder as she took a step toward the stage. "Nic. Wait. You don't have to do this. You have nothing to prove."

"I know. But who am I to deny these fine citizens the pleasure of seeing me dance?"

And with a wink, she climbed the stairs and stepped into the cage.

Chapter Five

A DAM ROUNDED ON his ex-girlfriend, his fists clenched. He'd never been tempted to hit a woman before, but she sure was pushing his buttons. "What the hell are you doing, Angela?"

"I'm putting miss high and mighty in her place." She twined her arms around his neck. "You are so out of her league, Adam. She's nothing but white trash. You should be thanking me for doing you a favor and showing you how she doesn't belong."

"What is *wrong* with you? Christ almighty." He extracted himself from the clutches of the clinging redhead. "Have the people in this town always been this judgmental, and I've just had my head so far up my ass I couldn't see it?" He turned and tried to make his way to the stage, but the crowd was already four people deep. "Nic. Nic!"

Criminy. No wonder Nic looked as if she'd swallowed a live bull frog when he brought her to The Crescent. And it also made sense as to why she was so gun-shy around people and insisted on being called Nic after hearing the way Angela said her name, as if "Nicolette" was something icky found on the bottom of her shoe. Was this how Nic had been treated all her life? Looked at with scorn just because she marched to the beat of her own drum? It sickened him to know that it was probably the case.

Even so, that didn't mean he needed to allow that kind of stupidity to continue.

"Nic!" he shouted, pushing his way closer to the staircase that led up to the stage.

She caught his gaze through the gaps between the wide slats of the cage and winked. With a rebel yell, she gestured to the DJ, who then cranked up the volume on the guitar wailing opening of "Bad Girlfriend" by Theory of a Dead Man.

The crowd went wild as Nic launched into a dance routine worthy of the finest burlesque show. She shimmied, she bounced, she jumped up and hung from the top of the cage, kicking her legs into positions Adam had only seen in strip clubs.

Torn between lust and fear for her safety, he watched as she whipped the crowd into a frenzy, moving with acrobatic skill as she climbed down and fell to her knees to twirl across the floor. She was sex incarnate as she temped and teased with a roll of her hips and shoulders. As Adam glanced around, he noticed every man gazed at Nic with passion glittering in their eyes as their girls looked on with envy.

"Holy shit," exclaimed one of the fellas crowding behind him. "Is that the chick from the bakery?"

"Oh yeah," his buddy answered. "I didn't realize she was so hot."

"Totally. I'd glaze her doughnuts any day."

"Shake that ass, girl," they shouted. "Shake that ass."

Adam rounded on them with a growl. "Shut the fuck up. That's my girl you're talking about."

"Seriously?" The taller of the two slapped him on the back. "You lucky bastard."

Another whoop from the crowd brought his attention back

to the stage, where Nic was now hanging from the outside of the cage, swiveling her body and encouraging people to spray their beers all over as if shooting water from a fire hose. As she tried to dodge the sprays of foam, she wore the biggest grin while she laughed and struck a pose as the song came to a whirlwind finish.

"All right, all right. Let's hear it for Nicolette," the DJ shouted over the thunderous applause.

Nic was helped down from the stage by a few admiring cowboys. Ignoring their attempts to keep her attention, she kept her gaze firmly on Adam as she passed a pissed-off Angela. Adam's ex fumed, with rage in her eyes and her hands clenched by her sides as beer dripped off the end of her nose. Guess that would teach her for trying to get an up close look at what she thought would be a train wreck.

"How was that?" Nic asked while her sweat glistened bosom heaved as she caught her breath.

"That was…ahhh." He lifted his hat to run his hand through his hair as his brain struggled to form a sentence. The words *claim* and *mine* flashed behind his closed eyes like a billboard on Times Square. "Damn, girl. All I can think to say right now is I really want to show you the flatbed of my truck."

Those wondrous breasts of hers bounced with her laughter. "Then let's go, cowboy."

His voice dropped an octave. "Are you sure? Because I wanna give you a real thorough tour."

The corner of her mouth curled up with a wicked tilt, and she curled her fingers around his belt buckle, brushing the hard length of his erection that was testing the integrity of his jeans. "What are we waiting for?"

Fuck yeah.

He grabbed her hand and all but hauled her out of the bar as she ran to keep up with his long-legged strides. When they reached his truck, he stopped short and spun to face her, pulling her close with his hands on her hips.

The shadow caused by the brim of his hat overtook her pretty face as he bent and took her lips in a kiss that had been brewing inside him all evening. Nic's lips parted with a sigh and she eagerly sucked his tongue into the cavern of her mouth. She was like a flame in his arms, hot, twisting, and burning him alive as she gave as good as she got.

He drew back with a gasp and his knees buckled as he gazed down into her sex-drugged eyes. "Last chance, Nic," he rasped. "I either take you home now, or we go someplace private. Someplace where I'm gonna want to see you naked. Then I'll want to touch you, and kiss you some more, and the night will probably end with us having sex. If you want something different, you best tell me now."

"You crack me up, cowboy." She placed a trail of kisses from the corner of his mouth to his ear. "Are you packing condoms?"

"Yes, ma'am."

"You were that sure of your chances?"

"Hopeful. I was extremely hopeful."

The hot puff of her laughter tickled his neck. "Show me what your idea of 'private' is and we'll see."

"Let's go, sweetness."

Chapter Six

ONCE THEY HIT the road, Adam wished he had actually planned on the "somewhere private" part of the evening. Obviously her place was out, and no way was he taking her back to his house with Rafe and Jack there. Renting a room for the night at the Inn was so skeevy, not to mention word about them would get around right quick once he checked them in.

Oh, wait. He knew the perfect spot. Not too far off the beaten path, beautiful scenery, and best of all, private.

He turned off the main road to a dirt path that led through a growth of fir trees.

"Is this where you take me into the woods to hide my body?" Nic asked.

"Of course not. If I were going to murder you, I'd take you back to the ranch, grind up your body and feed it to the herd."

He loved the way she giggled. The tone was deep and raspy and sounded in no way girlish. "I am both amused and horrified you had an answer so readily at hand."

"When you're out in the field for several hours a day, sometimes all on your own, your brain wanders."

"I can tell." Her smile flashed white in the near dark, and he answered in kind as they broke past the tree line.

"Paradise, madam," he said and pulled the truck to a stop on a small cliff overlooking the rushing river.

"Where are we?" she asked as she climbed down.

"This is where the Canyon River cuts into my parents' ranch. Since the hillside is so steep, they can't use it for grass land, but they have water rights, which irrigates most of the north end of the property. When my brothers and I were younger, we'd inner tube from a spot a mile upstream and pull out here where we'd have a couple of ATVs waiting for us."

"Sounds cold."

"But on days like today when it's a hundred degrees out, it don't matter. Come on, you can't tell me you've never been tubing down the Canyon."

"Nope. Never."

He drew up short with his hand on the tailgate. "Now that is just about the saddest thing I ever heard. Before the summer is over. You and me. We're tubing down the river."

"Good luck with that, cowboy," she said with a laugh.

"Oh, it's as good as done, sweet cheeks. Now give me a minute here."

From the chest in the back of his truck, he withdrew a foam roll-up and a sleeping bag that he laid out across the flatbed.

"It's not the most comfortable of surfaces, but it'll be softer than the ground," he said as he held out his hand to help her climb up.

"You have quite the setup. Do you woo girls out in the open like this often?"

"Well, um…"

Damn. Why did the mere thought of speaking of his past relationships make him want to hide in the deepest, darkest cave? Maybe it was because Nic had just come face to face with his crazy ex not more than half an hour prior, and what a stellar moment that had been. Way to show he was an excellent judge of character.

But his embarrassment went deeper than that. For some reason he didn't want Nic to think that he thought of her as just another date or potential girlfriend. There was something special brewing between them, and he didn't want the specter of an old standby tainting their budding relationship.

"I wouldn't say that," he stuttered. "I've been with girls here before. Not like this, but you know, tubing. And I've been outdoors with girls, necking and stuff. But not a lot of girls. Some. Few. Less than ten. I think."

Nic stopped him by placing her hand across his mouth as she doubled over with laughter. "Oh my God. You have to stop before I pee my pants. It wasn't an inquisition. It was a joke."

"Ha ha. Funny. Look, Nic, I just don't want you to think that this is just part of my routine. My normal seduction."

"And you think that's important to me? That I'll care if I'm just another girl?"

"It's important to me. And yes, I think it is to you, too. But you're too cool to admit it." He tapped her on her cute nose. "If I had to guess, I'd say you have had people tell you to stop being different so many times that you are now at the point where you embrace it and would hate being considered ordinary in any way."

With a light harrumph, she folded her arms over her chest. "That is quite the observation there, cowboy."

And dead-on accurate, if the pout of her lips said anything.

"I don't think you're weird, Nic. Or ordinary. I think you are extraordinarily special."

Her pout softened into a smile, and in the moonlight she reminded him of a siren or some other magical creature as she sat on the makeshift bed and laid on her back.

"Not so bad," she said and patted the spot beside her. "The stars are gorgeous tonight."

He placed his hat on top of the cab and lay down next to her. "Prettier than they are in Paris?"

"Yes. Less light pollution here."

The moment he settled into place, she lifted his arm and scooted closer until all of her luscious curves were pressed along his side and her head rested on his chest.

Ah…now this was the life right there. The soft rustle of the river rolling by, a glorious night sky, and a beautiful, sexy woman nestled in your arms. It didn't get much better than that.

"Nic," he whispered, not wanting to disrupt the peacefulness of their surroundings more than necessary. "I'm sorry about The Crescent. I wouldn't have taken you if I knew you had a past there."

When she laughed, her entire body vibrated against him. "I don't really have a past. Megan has a past. I was an innocent—okay, maybe not so innocent bystander. It was fun tonight. For a while, anyway."

"Yeah. I'm sorry about Angela, too. I knew she could be bitchy, but I didn't realize she could be a Godzilla-sized vindictive bitch."

"How long ago did you break up?"

"Last April."

"It appears as if she hasn't gotten over you. Why did you end it?"

"Besides the obvious bitchiness?" He started to laugh, but as he gazed into her eyes, he felt his stomach twist as he thought about his relationship with Angela.

It shamed him to admit that the main reason he went out with Angela, and continued to do so for so long, was because she was pretty and popular. Their peer group had expected them to be a couple, and so they were. Too many times, he had let her snide comments or rude behavior slide because she looked good on his arm. And it was only when she started to make him change to be more like her, or her version of him, was when he had decided to end it.

Realizing you were a shallow person was a bitter pill to swallow, and his throat ached as he tried to form the words. "She wasn't what I wanted out of life. As a partner. I wasn't my best when I was with her. So I ended things."

"Sounds like you made the right decision."

"Wish I made it sooner." A lot, lot sooner.

She shrugged. "Could have been worse. You could still be dating. Or married."

Talk about giving him the willies. "No. That ship has long sailed. And I'm looking for greener pastures. Someone I can be myself with. Have fun. But also keep me in line and responsible, but in a nice way."

Nic smiled and snuggled deeper against his side. "I hope you find her."

"Thanks," he replied then pulled back in surprise.

Wait. What?

"You don't think that girl is you?"

"Are you kidding? You are destined to settle down with little Suzie Homemaker, have five or six kids, and stay in Mission forever. That girl is not me. My path is out there in the great wide somewhere. As soon as—well, as soon as things with the bakery are smoothed out, I'm outta here. I am your diversion until you find the girl of your dreams."

Well, he *had* been thinking Nic was the girl of his dreams, until she burst his bubble.

But even with her firm resolution that he was going to be able to let her walk away, he still believed she might be the one.

And the thought of her leaving, or thinking she was going to be nothing more than a fling, was almost as depressing as his relationship with Angela.

"Is that so," he rasped. "And when are you planning on leaving?"

"Not sure yet." She toyed with the snaps of his shirt. "Could be a few months. Maybe a year."

A year, huh? Then he still had time to convince her to stay around and explore more of the magic he felt igniting between them. Maybe even convince her to stay and become his girl.

"What will you do then?" he asked. "Go back to Paris? New York? Or someplace else where you can use your wicked dance skills? Criminy, girl. Those were some seriously hot moves. Where did you learn to dance like that?"

She giggled and snuggled closer. "Megan and I took a strip-tease class our first year out on our own. Let me tell you, there is nothing more humbling than having a drag queen show you how to dance in four-inch platforms and make it look easy."

"A drag queen taught you how to strip?"

"It was more of a burlesque class than stripping. Although he did show us some cool moves on the pole. That's a lot of work. Huh. Maybe I should get back to it. Lose some of this baking weight."

"Don't you dare," he gasped in outrage. "I like your curves. In fact, my palms are itching to become more acquainted with them."

"Are they?" she cooed and her lips brushed against his. "Prove it."

"Yes, ma'am."

With fevered kisses he kissed her smile away as his hands went to town on her hips and the sweet curve of her ass, hauling her over him until she was laying half on top of him.

Nic speared her fingers into his hair and scraped little circles on his scalp with her nails. Then those magical fingers of hers trailed down his chest, where she scored lines from his sternum to the barrier of his belt.

"Lord almighty, woman," he gasped as he came up for air. "Everything you do is so damn sexy. The way you move. The way you breathe. I've never been so turned on in my life."

"Thank you. That's sweet," she replied in that way women do that made him think she didn't believe him. Especially when she looked away with a flutter of her lashes.

"Don't be that way, sweetness. I mean it." He shifted his hips and pressed the hard length of his erection against her soft belly. "I'm afraid I'm going to embarrass myself any second."

She laughed. "And if you do, are you done for the night? Will you fall asleep and I'll have to drive you home?"

"Nah. With the proper encouragement, I'll be ready again in no time. But still, shooting off too soon doesn't make for a good showing."

"Hmmm." She bit her lip and her brow furrowed. "Let me be the judge of that."

She lowered her head and took his lips in a kiss that sent fire racing through his veins. His bones melted and he lay there, a hapless mass of male need as he allowed her to plunder his mouth as she saw fit. Like a musician strumming a guitar, she ran her hands over his chest and under his shirt, stroking his belly until he became intoxicated with her taste and touch. It was as if she were the sun and he a lazy ol' tomcat basking in the heat of her rays.

But he didn't want to just cruise on the tide of her attention like a leaf floating on the surface of the river. He wanted to be the rock that altered the course and impacted the river forever.

Nic talked a good game, but he'd seen enough during the

evening to recognize that deep down she had the same insecurities a good chunk of the female population struggled with. If he had it in his power to make her see herself the way he did, he was going to do his damnedest to convince her she was perfect.

"This is your last chance, Miss Nicolette," he said against her lips as he gripped the hem of her blouse. "Once I start, I'm not gonna want to stop."

"If you haven't noticed, I'm a sure thing, cowboy. Now stop talking and take me already."

He tipped his head back with a laugh. "So impatient. Sorry, sweetness, I've been looking forward to this night all week. No way am I going to rush this."

At least that was his plan until he got her shirt up and over her head. Beneath her blouse Nic wore a sheer, black mesh bra that did nothing to hide the pebbled tips of her dusky nipples. Before he thought better of it, he swiped the back of his hand over his lips as his mouth began to water.

"Lord almighty," he breathed. "Does your love of French things include fancy lace underwear?"

Her smile widened. "I'll show you mine if you show me yours."

"Done." He tore his shirt open and flung it aside to land who knew where. His white cotton tank followed, sailing over the side of the truck while Nic got to her feet on the flatbed and unbuttoned her jeans.

Moonlight kissed her skin with a golden glow as the material slid down her legs, and again he couldn't help but think of Nic as some fairytale creature he had been fortunate enough to capture, if only for a moment.

"You like?" she asked and turned in a careful circle before dropping to her knees before him. Matching black mesh panties with black silk ribbons running down the fabric encased her rounded hips and backside, teasing him with glimpses of the creamy skin beneath.

"I love." Damn. He was going to need a bib before long. "Lie down here and let me drink you in."

"Drink me in. The way you phrase things cracks me up."

"Well, that's what I plan on doing. I have a friend who told me that the best sex was when you took the time to learn your partner. What turned them on, how they moved, the sounds they made. Give them everything they wanted and then some. Scoot this way," he instructed. "That's it. Right in the moonlight. Fuck, Nic, you are so beautiful. I'm going to do more than drink you in. I'm going to absorb you. Feast on you until we pass out with gluttonous hangovers."

Tears glimmered in her eyes before she blinked them away. She raised her hands above her head and arched into a seductive pose. "Then feast away, cowboy."

The way his hands shook as he reached for her made him giddy. He had meant it when he said he had never been so turned on in his life. Not even when it had been his first time with a woman.

There was just something about Nic that was different. That made everything he felt and thought mean something more, special, epic somehow. It was as if for the first time he understood what it meant to be a man. A man who was set on pleasing his woman and bringing her so much pleasure, she was going to be reduced to a quivering, sated heap of womanhood by the time he was through.

That thought made him smile as he tugged the strap of her bra down her arm with one hand while reaching behind her with the other. The clasp gave way with ease, and seconds later, her creamy breasts spilled into his hands.

"Forgive me, sweetness," he rasped as he gently squeezed

her generous breasts. "But I gotta."

And with that he buried his face between the soft mounds and rubbed his cheeks against her silky flesh.

Nic let loose with a peal of laughter and hugged him around the shoulders. "You've been wanting to do that all night, haven't you?"

"Yes, ma'am." He sighed and settled in deeper to enjoy the beat of her heart against his cheek. "This right here is heaven."

She hummed with contentment and ran her fingers through his hair. "This is nice."

Nice? *Nice?* Hell, he didn't want just nice. He wanted to be the best she ever had.

"Then I guess I need to try harder to impress you," he said, then sucked a puckered nipple between his lips.

Her back arched as she hissed. "Oh. That's a good start."

"Damn straight."

The hills and valleys of her body were a delight to his senses. Working in a bakery must have changed her body chemistry, for he swore he scented vanilla on her skin, and she tasted like salted caramel as he licked his way over her succulent breasts and down the rounded mound of her belly.

"You are so soft," he murmured against her hip as he slipped her lacy panties down her thighs. "You remind me of that stuff you put over your cakes to make it all smooth and perfect."

"Fondant?" she asked with a laugh. "I hope not. Really, that stuff is inedible."

"Well, then, I guess that's where you're different, because I'm gonna gobble you all up."

Her sex was drenched, a well of honey that was ambrosia against his tongue as he licked and nibbled her feminine folds. She bucked her hips and her fingers wound into his hair, guiding him to exactly where she wanted his mouth.

"Yes. God, yes. Right there," she panted and tugged on his hair.

He couldn't hold back a smile as she made no secret about how best to please her. Of course, he was a willing student, eager to learn where to stroke, where to bite, how deep to sink his fingers into her sheath to make her whimper for more.

Just as her channel began to tighten around his fingers, he pulled away and lifted to his knees.

"No," she cried. "Why did you stop?"

"One second longer and this bull is going to be castrated," he replied and attacked the fly of his jeans.

His aching cock burst free and he groaned with the release of pressure. The seconds it took to roll the condom down his shaft were almost as torturous as the time spent being strangled by the constricting fabric.

It took his last bit of control to keep from falling on her like a rabid animal, but the long slow glide of his cock into her sheath was worth every second as he sank into her heat.

"Look at me, sweetness," he said as her eyelids fluttered shut. "I wanna look into your beautiful eyes."

That slow, sinful grin of hers curled her lips as she wrapped her legs around his waist and squeezed. "Come on, cowboy. Ride me."

He laughed and all of his tension dissipated like grains of sand in a windstorm. Oh, he was still hard as a rock and a hair's breadth away from shooting hard and deep inside her, but his expectation to be the end-all, be-all of her sexual history was gone, replaced by the sheer pleasure of being with Nic. Of enjoying the intimacy of skin on skin contact as he rocked against her.

Soon, the truck began to sway as the thrust of his hips gained power and Nic responded with a roll of her own. She scored the tips of her nails down his back, up and down, digging deeper with each pass as her pussy grew tighter and tighter around him.

Her lashes fluttered as she clenched her teeth. "Right there. Just like that. If you stop this time, I will punch you in the throat, I swear to God."

Was there ever a time when he laughed so much while having sex? While having hot, amazing sex? When had he ever felt such joy being with another person?

Wow, he realized. Never.

Since she had asked so sweetly, he concentrated on repeating the same action over and over as she turned into a live wire beneath him, thrashing and growling until her eyes widened and she gasped, shaking hard with an orgasm that kicked him closer to the edge of oblivion. Sweat trickled into his eyes, but he didn't dare stop as her body heaved and pitched, until at long last her moans quieted and she looked up at him, drowsy, sated.

And then she laughed.

No. She giggled. A melodic sound of unadulterated glee that skipped over his skin, down his spine, and out into the universe. It was as if he had been living all his life in a haze, and with her laughter, that dome shattered, revealing the wonders of the world. His hearing sharpened, honing in on the rush of the river and the squeak of the shocks of his truck as he lunged faster and faster.

The scent of apples ripening from a nearby orchard mingled with the musky scent of their sex. And Nic's eyes, lord almighty, Nic's eyes sparkled like the gleam off a silver buckle.

"Holy shit," he groaned, lost in the beauty around him, and came hard, pouring himself into the woman beneath him. A creature who possessed such magic, she changed his view of the world forever.

"Oh my God," he moaned, over and over as he collapsed at her side and gathered her into his arms.

Nicolette Fournier.

He knew it. He knew it from the moment he first laid eyes on her.

She was The One.

Chapter Seven

A DAM CLIMBED THE front steps of Nic's house and paused to take a few deep breaths to quell the roiling sensation in his gut. Damn, he hadn't been so nervous about knocking on a girl's front door since his second date with his first girlfriend.

Emily Reynolds. Eighth grade. He hadn't known he was supposed to be nervous when he had gone to pick her up after the first time. He had asked her out. She had said yes. Awesome. The hard part was already over.

Then her father answered the door. All six-foot-four of burly Norwegian rancher who then grilled him on everything from what television shows he watched to what video games he played. He had even asked if Adam knew how to perform CPR. Apparently his answers had been acceptable since he was allowed to take Emily out for a second date, but his hand had been a whole lot shakier the next time he had come around and rung the doorbell.

Of course, he wouldn't now be standing on Nic's porch like a dweeb with his stomach in knots if he were certain his appearance was going to be a welcomed sight.

A day was far too long to go without seeing her pretty face, which made the last week and a half torture. With the ranch getting ready to bring a portion of their stock to market, and Nic being up to her eyeballs in graduation cakes, the short phone calls they had been able to squeeze in during their busy schedule were but a small appetizer, and he was starved for more of Nic's loving. Especially when she sent him sexy text messages. Oh boy, could that girl text. They were like the most sinfully dark chocolate truffles and he consumed them by the pound.

Never before had he been a slave to his phone, but now he couldn't leave the thing out of his sight. Mark said if he caught him with the phone in his hand one more time while out in the field, he'd shove it up the nearest cow's ass. And he'd do it too.

So with the boss man up his ass, that had left Adam counting the hours until he was able to sneak away and ask her out for a proper date.

And she had said no.

"No? What do you mean, 'No'?" he had asked. "It's only dinner."

And on a Tuesday night.

In Mission.

What other plans could she possibly have?

"Yeah, it's been a long day. And I'm sure you have lots of other things you'd rather be doing. Maybe some other time."

"Nic, what's wrong? You sound funny."

"It's fine. I'm fine." She heaved an exasperated sigh. "Just stuff, and life, and shit. Look, Adam, I have to go."

Fine, huh? Then why did his gut clench at the stress he heard in her voice? "Call me, okay? Later tonight when it's quiet. I don't care what time it is."

"Maybe. We'll see. Gotta go."

For several moments he had stared at the silent phone in his hand until Jack knocked him on the shoulder with a warning that Mark was approaching. The suspicion that all was not right in his girl's world nagged him like a burr in his boot. The second he had finished with his work, he hopped in his truck and headed for town.

Sure, Nic said she was fine, but he had to see for himself that she was okay.

And if she were with another guy?

Well, that would be an altogether different issue. And still something that was best settled in person.

He wiped his damp palm on his jeans, then shifted the bouquet of flowers he carried to do the same with the other hand. When intruding on a woman's free time, Colby suggested he may want to bring something pretty, and Adam agreed.

"It'll be fine," he muttered. "She'll be happy to see you."

He hoped.

The doorbell chimed and he waited. And waited. And waited some more as sweat began to collect along his forehead. He extended his hand to the button again when the door flew open.

The woman who stood at the threshold was the spitting image of Nic. Well, Nic in about thirty years. Thick streaks of silver ran through her shoulder-length dark hair and she sported wrinkles around her eyes and mouth, but her lips, nose, and eyes were exact copies of Nic's. An oversized blue T-shirt with the Seahawks logo hung on her thin frame to her knees, and black leggings clung to her calves and stopped at her bare feet.

"Hello," he said. "Is Nic home?"

She batted her eyes in confusion for a moment before a huge smile curled her lips. "Angus Maguire. I didn't know you had a play date with Nicolette. Did your mother drop you off?" She popped up on her tiptoes to look over his shoulder.

"No, ma'am." He cocked his head and frowned. "I brought myself."

"Ooo. Look at you, you're getting to be such a big boy,

riding your bike all the way from the ranch. Well, come in, come in. We're letting all of the hot air in the house."

As he crossed the threshold, the eeriest sense of what-the-hell stole over him and had him looking in the corners of the room for hidden cameras.

"Nic," she shouted up the staircase. "Angus Maguire is here. Why didn't you remind me you had a play date?"

"Actually, ma'am," he interjected. "I'm Adam. Angus is my brother."

"Adam?" Her lashes fluttered like the wings of a butterfly. "That's impossible. Adam is just a baby."

"Not any more. I'm twenty-four now."

"Twenty-four?" The frown lines on her brow smoothed even as tears filled her eyes. "Twenty-four? No. That can't be. You're a baby. I made your first birthday cake just the other week."

"I'm sorry, ma'am, but you must be thinking of someone else."

"No. I remember." Her hair flew in all directions as she shook her head. "It was a large rectangle of Winnie the Pooh dressed as a cowboy. And the side one for you was a red balloon with a gold star."

Damn, she was right. He might have been a baby at the time, but he'd seen the pictures of his first birthday many times, especially the ones with the little balloon cake his mother had ordered just for him. More cake had made it all over his face and high chair than in his mouth, and his skin had been stained a ruddy shade of pink from the food coloring in the icing for several days.

"That's right. But it wasn't last week." And at that, she let out a wail and began to pace back and forth. "But we can pretend it was. That's fine by me."

"Mom? What were you saying?" Nic's voice came from upstairs, followed quickly by the sound of her feet hitting the stairs at a rapid clip. She pulled up short when she spotted them in the living room. "Oh."

Gone was the heavy black eyeliner and red lipstick he was used to as she stared at him with her face scrubbed free of cosmetics. Her hair hung in wet, wavy strands, and her T-shirt clung to parts of her body in wet patches.

Free from the mask of her makeup, Nic appeared softer, and much more vulnerable as horror widened her eyes and her lower lip began to tremble in the same manner as the other woman's had just a moment before.

"Adam," Nic whispered. "What are you doing here?"

"I came to take you to dinner."

"Dinner? What? No. I—I can't. God." She closed her eyes and heaved a big sigh. "Mother." She dashed past him to stand nose to nose to the sobbing woman and settled her hands on the other woman's shoulders. "Mom. Mom. Can you tell me what the ingredients are in frangipane? I can't remember."

"What, darling? Frangipane?" Her mother's sobs slowed to a hiccup and she batted her eyes again. "That's your grandfather's favorite."

"I know. Can you remind me what's in it?"

"You remember. Butter, eggs, sugar, and almond paste."

"Oh, yeah. That's right. And what about cherries jubilee?"

"That's your favorite."

"I know. What are the ingredients?"

"Butter, brown sugar, cherries, salt, bourbon, and ice cream. French vanilla ice cream."

"That sounds delicious. Thank you for reminding me." She gave her mother a hug. "Aunt Jacqui will have dinner ready soon. Are you hungry?"

"Yes. So hungry." Her mother wiped her nose with the hem of her shirt.

"Good. Hey, I have a friend coming over. Would you like to meet him?"

"Him?" Her brown eyes sparkled as she smiled, and for the first time Adam noticed the right side of her face appeared more lax than the left. "Would this be a boyfriend?"

"Well, he's a boy." Nic placed her arm around her mother's shoulders and turned her to face him. "Mom, this is Adam. Adam, my mother, Marie."

"It's a pleasure to meet you, ma'am." He held out his hand, unsure if he should even dare make a move. Clearly Marie Fournier was not at one hundred percent, but the how and why was far beyond his level of experience or comprehension.

"Oh, so polite. He even brought flowers." Marie giggled and shook his hand. "And he's handsome, too."

Was that a smile or a grimace from Nic as she said, "Yes, he is. Why don't you go see what Aunt Jacqui is doing in the kitchen?"

"I think she's making dinner." Marie turned to him. "Will you be joining us, Adam? Please say you will."

"I'd—"

"Adam can't stay, Mom. He just dropped by to say a quick hello on his way through town."

"No. He *will* stay." Marie pouted. "I insist. And he will sit by me."

Nic's lips tightened and her nostrils flared as she grunted in that way his sisters-in-law did when their kids started acting up. Truth be told, he didn't know who Nic was more frustrated with, her mother or him.

While it was always a good idea to score points with the parental unit, he'd rather dissolve Nic's anger and keep in her good graces.

"I'm sorry, Mrs. Fournier," he said, handing her the bouquet of roses. "I am just on my way through town and stopped by to say a quick hello. Maybe another time."

"Isn't that sweet." Marie buried her nose into the petals and inhaled. "I know this type, don't I?"

"Yes," Nic replied with a rasp in her voice. "They're called Clarion's Call."

Marie's eyes flashed. "You like these ones."

"I do. They're my favorite." She paused to clear her throat. "Will you ask Jacqui to put them in some water?"

"Okay." Marie spun on her heel and disappeared through the door without a look back.

"I'm sorry, Nic," he said the moment they were alone. "I didn't know—"

She stopped him with a lift of her hand. "Not here."

The resigned crinkle in her brow and the way she avoided eye contact with him as she led him to the front porch set his stomach roiling again. At this rate, he might have to buy a case of antacid on his way home.

Concern over the future of their relationship turned into concern for Nic's well-being as the front porch light emphasized the dark circles under her eyes. His girl was tired, bone tired. But before he gave into the temptation to mention her appearance, her lips twisted in that determined way of hers, and she finally looked up to meet his gaze.

"Adam—"

No. He had to speak his peace first. "I'm sorry I turned up out of the blue. Really, Nic. I've just missed you so much and I thought what harm could come from taking you out to dinner? I didn't think."

Her shoulders drooped, and despite it being a balmy eighty-five degrees, she wrapped her arms around her chest as if she were cold. She worried her lower lip between her teeth and took several breaths before she sighed. "Today...was not a good day."

Hedging his bets that she wasn't kicking him to the curb, he sat on the top of the low porch wall and held his tongue.

Nic sighed again. "Just over a year ago, my mother had a stroke. Not too long afterward, she started to exhibit signs of dementia. Lack of focus, loss of memory, changes in personality, hallucinations. Her condition has been growing steadily worse."

"That's why she didn't believe who I was. She thought I was my brother."

"The fact that she remembers your family at all is a miracle." She turned to look over her shoulder at the closed front door, squinting as if she could see through the oak to the other side. "And she recognized my favorite flower. Earlier today she couldn't remember much of anything and fought me all day long on simple things from eating breakfast to brushing her hair. We have a caregiver who comes a few days a week. Aunt Jacqui and I watch her the rest of the time. It's an all-day event. Just when you think you can take a minute to squeeze in a shower, she goes and opens the door to let a stranger into the house," she added with a lopsided smile aimed in his direction.

"I really am sorry I intruded, Nic. I didn't know what you were living with."

She shrugged and joined him at the railing. "It's not easy to tell people that your mother is losing her mind. Whether it's dementia or mental illness, it's all so complex, no two people have the exact same experiences, which makes it difficult to prepare for those differences. And on top of all of that is the sad reality that there is no cure. Whatever issues you have, you will have for the rest of your life. All you can really do is manage your symptoms, but they'll never truly go away. Every day you wake up never knowing if you are going to be in control of your thoughts and actions. A logical mind could at any moment behave illogically, therefore everyone who comes into contact with that person is affected. Chaos creators. You never know how and to what extreme, but it's an undeniable truth." She paused and looked down to where she was tapping at a knot in the wood slat of the porch floor with her big toe. "And the general public is afraid of that chaos and lump anything related to the brain and an imbalance in one scary pool, so there's a stigma on those who battle the condition. So yeah, I don't talk about my mother much."

The need to apologize, again, burned his lips, but he didn't dare utter the words. After all, that was all they were. Words.

He'd been blessed with a life where strife was an infrequent guest. A charmed life, some would say. And he'd agree. Just listening to what Nic faced day in and day out exhausted him. He couldn't imagine walking in her shoes, watching the woman who raised you slip away a little bit each day without the hope she would ever return.

But if there was one thing he learned while working at the Sprawling A, it was that you never gave up on hope. Even in the hardest of struggles, the will to persevere could create miracles.

"There is nothing that can be done to help your mom?" he asked. "Some type of therapy or something?"

"As I said, we manage. There is nothing that will stop the dementia from getting worse. We just take things day by day. The caregiver helps, and I wish we could afford her to be here full time, but that's pricey. There are a few specialists in the city, but again, expensive. Look, I know that what we're doing now is a Band-Aid. Before I know it, we won't be able to manage having Mom here at all. Then we'll have to send her to a hospital or group home. I really don't want to have her institutionalized, but soon, we may not have a choice."

A sparkle appeared on her cheek, then another. The tiny starbursts held him entranced until he realized it was the reflection of the setting sun in the tears slipping down her face.

Watching a woman break down in tears was not a new concept for him, but this was Nic. Nic was strong. Nic was a badass who threw a giant middle finger up to anything or anyone out to cause her strife. If Nic was brought to tears, the world was going down in flames.

Of course, Nic didn't cry like anyone he'd ever seen. She didn't make a sound. Not even her breath stuttered. There was only the silent tremble of her lips and the silvery tracks coursing down her face. An ache blossomed in his chest and his heart broke as he watched her silently bear the weight of the world on her shoulders.

"Come here, sweetness." He scooped her up and hauled her against his side, drawing her legs over his lap to hold her close.

"I'm sorry," she mumbled into his chest. "Just ignore me. I'm fine."

"Hush that talk." He rubbed his palms up and down her back as she shuddered. "You're entitled to your feelings. And if I know you like I think I do, you've been bottling them up for a long time." He drew back enough to tilt her chin up with his fingers and smooth the tears away with his thumb. "So if you've been spending all of your time taking care of your mom and the business, who's taking care of you?"

She snorted with a laugh. "I take care of myself."

"That's what I thought. Well, not anymore. I'm going to take care of you."

"Adam—"

"No, no. Hear me out. You can't take on everything by yourself. You'll crack. I've seen it. Before I started working at the A, Trey and Greta's son died. Trey let the loss consume him, and it sucked him into a hole we didn't think he'd ever come out of, but Greta fought the sadness. She let us be there for her. Even if all we did was sit in the same room and let her cook for us. Then again, I'd never let an opportunity go by to have some of Greta's cooking. But the point is, she needed support, and we gave it to her. Trey refused and it took him almost dying to realize what it was he was missing out on. Let me be there for you, Nic. Give you a hand, or support, whatever you need. You don't have to do this alone."

"I appreciate the gesture, but I'm not your responsibility, Adam."

"I'm making you mine. Ha." He barked with laughter. "I'm making *you mine*. I guess I didn't make it clear the other night when I shouted your name in orgasmic pleasure, but I like you, Nic. A lot. I don't want to just date you. I want you to be my girl. I want to make you smile. I want to hold you when you're sad. Let me be your rock and give you what no one else can. Please."

More tears tumbled down her cheeks as she buried her face against his chest. Through the fabric of his shirt, he felt the hot puffs of her breath shuddering past her lips, but she still didn't make a sound as she wept in his arms.

Nic was a proud woman. To allow him to witness her at a time of weakness spoke to him the depth of her need. To be held. Hell, he'd hold her forever if she'd let him. But she was Nic, after all, and before he was ready to part, she controlled her breathing and tried to pull away.

"You're too much, Adam Maguire." She sniffed. "Just too much."

"But you like me anyway."

"Yeah. I do."

Funny. He had thought she was beautiful with the moonlight bathing her naked body, but with the sun setting behind her, making her eyes look like pools of milk chocolate and her lips like raspberries, she was stunning.

The urge to taste her compelled him forward with a power that could not be denied. Her kiss was as sweet as she looked, even sweeter. And so damn soft, he wanted to sink inside her and stay forever. The damp strands of her hair were cool against the back of his fingers as he cupped her neck and angled her just so to deepen the kiss to a level so hot, sweat began to trickle from his hairline.

"Nicolette. Nicolette!" her mother shouted through the front window as she pounded on the glass. "Don't forget to use condoms."

"Thanks, Mom," Nic replied with a wave, then climbed off his lap.

"I guess that's my cue to leave," he said with a husky chuckle and stood, taking a moment to adjust the fit of his jeans. "Have a good night, Nic."

"Adam." She reached for his hand. Her chest rose as she drew in a deep breath. "Would you like to join my family for dinner?"

"Yeah?" He tried to temper his joy at having her welcome him into her family circle, but he couldn't stop the huge grin from stretching his lips. "I'd like that a lot."

"Good." She tugged on his hand and led him to the front door.

Step two: Meet the parents. Check. Well, mostly checked. She had yet to meet the Maguire clan in full force. A daunting prospect indeed.

In fact, if it was a competition between the stress of having dinner with Marie and her dementia or dinner with his clan? A night at the Fourniers' was going to be a piece of cake.

Chapter Eight

A KNOCK ON the front door of his house brought Adam's head around as he was finishing up his morning shave. Early-morning visitors were not that rare, but usually if someone wanted something from one of the guys, they'd call or send a text.

"Is anyone expecting company?" Rafe asked on his way to the living room.

Both Adam and Jack answered in the negative as they joined him, more curious to see who it was than anything. Their house was a long way off the road, so someone would have to be pretty serious if they wanted to do them harm. Then again, they'd had their share of trauma on the ranch, so anything was possible.

Rafe eased open the door, then jerked it wide open as he recognized their guest. "Mrs. Maguire. This is a surprise."

"Good morning, Rafael." Beverly crossed the threshold and lifted her cheek to Rafe, who bussed it in greeting. "Ooo, you smell good."

"Mom?" Adam stood there, shell-shocked in his boots. "What are you doing here?"

"If my son won't come see me, then I'll come see my son."

"But it's four-thirty in the morning."

Good lord. What time did she wake up to appear at his door so early with her long hair plaited in a nice braid and blush on her cheeks? He had just rolled out of bed right into the shower no more than ten minutes prior.

"I'm well aware what time a cowboy's day starts, Adam Patrick." She lifted the tote she had slung over her shoulder to chest level. "I thought we could have breakfast together and catch up."

Adam ignored his roommates' amused snorts. "Ah, gee, Ma. I was just about to head to the main house for breakfast with the rest of the guys."

"Then you haven't eaten yet. Perfect."

"What's wrong? Who died?" he asked, because something was most definitely going on. His mother *never* dropped in on him unexpectedly. Ever. Like never ever.

"Nothing's wrong. I just wanted to spend some time with my little sweet pea," she cooed, squishing his cheeks between her palms.

"Ah, Ma. Not in front of the guys."

"Don't mind us," Jack sputtered between laughs. "We were just heading out. Enjoy your breakfast, Ms. Beverly. And we'll see you out in the field, sweet pea."

"Let me go put on a shirt," Adam grumbled and stalked to his room with the sound of his roommates' departing laughter following him. He'd bet the twenty in his wallet that every man on the ranch was going to call him "sweet pea" before the end of the day.

He loved his mother, he truly did, but boy howdy did the woman know how to cut a man down to size.

"If I'd known you were going to come over," he said after he dressed, "I'd have tidied up some."

"Sure you would've," she replied in a tone that suggested

doubt of his claim. She pushed aside game controllers and picked up a few empties that were scattered across the coffee table. "At least it doesn't smell like dirty socks and rotten food. Don't you fellas ever want to entertain a lady here?"

"We do." He followed her in to the kitchen and lifted the lid on the recycle bin for her. "But the girls call us ahead of time so we can clean."

"Well, I'm your mother. I shouldn't have to schedule an appointment to see you." She set her bag on the counter and fired the oven right up. "I brought an egg and cheese casserole, some biscuits, and some fruit. This'll take a few minutes to warm up, which will give us plenty of time to chat."

"Okay, what's going on? If you wanted to talk, you could've called me."

"It's not the same." Beverly floated around the kitchen, pulling out dishes and glasses to set the small dining table. "I miss your face. You haven't been at a family dinner in weeks."

"I've been busy, Ma. I've told you."

"Busy doing what? And don't say working. You've been spotted downtown by your brothers many times. Admit it, you've been busy with Nic Fournier."

Busted by the bros. Of course.

"Yes, I've been seeing Nic. You knew that."

"But this sounds like something more than an occasional date. Is it getting serious?"

Question of the year, and he wish he knew the answer.

Nic was a ready and willing woman for just about anything, and by "anything," that meant activities of both the clean and dirty kind. That was until talk of the future came up. And to Nic, "the future" appeared to be anything that was planned for more than a few months out. Distress would flash in her eyes and her smile would freeze at an awkward slant until she found a way to change the subject. His girl was definitely good at keeping her thoughts close to the vest, but he noticed her hesitation.

"It's serious enough to know I want more from her," he answered and swiped his hand down his face. "But she has a lot going on at home. Do you know about her mother?"

"I've heard rumors, but I haven't seen Marie in years. She had a stroke some time back, yes?"

"Yeah." He accepted a glass of juice she had poured from the carton she had brought with her in her Mary Poppins bag and stared into the orange liquid. "Physically, she's doing pretty well, but since then she's developed signs of dementia."

"Ah, poor thing."

"So Nic and her aunt have their hands full. If I want to see more of Nic, then I have to go to where she is, which means lots of dinners in and movie rentals."

Beverly took the casserole out of the oven and set a piping hot plate of sausage, eggs, and cheesy goodness on the table before him, then took the seat to his left. "Is that where you've been these last few weeks? At Nic's?"

"Yup."

"And is Marie with you the entire time while you're there?"

"Most of the time. Sometimes she goes to bed early if it's been a trying day. When she's lucid, she's great. Funny. Very quick witted. But the bad days, boy, they can be something. I don't see how Nic and her aunt stay as positive as they do. Oh, they do have outside help on occasion, but it's mostly the two of them."

"So if you and Nic were to, say...get married," and with this, a delighted spark twinkled in his mother's eyes. "Would you be willing to take on some of the work in taking care of Marie? I can imagine that is a big responsibility."

To care for another, making sure they were well provided for and happy was a huge responsibility. It was one thing if it was your child, and an entirely different set of complications when it was the person who created you, birthed you, and kept you safe.

He understood Nic's duty to her family, he honestly did. That was why he happily passed up nights out at The Crescent or dinner at Stuart's in exchange for spaghetti dinners and action adventure movies. All he wanted was to spend time with Nic. It didn't matter where or what they were doing as long as they were together.

And if caring for her mother was part of being with Nic, then he'd do so with joy. Even though at times her mother's behavior was exhausting to the point of contemplating crawling inside a keg of beer and taking up residence.

"I've been giving some thought to that, but yes, of course. Her family would become my family. Man, this is good, Mom." He shoveled in a few more forkfuls of casserole and washed it down with a big gulp of juice. "Say, this is the dish you make for Christmas morning, right?"

"That's right."

Uh-oh. Surprise visit with her special, holiday-only meal. His mother *was* up to something.

"How's everyone on the ranch?" he asked, with a dash of suspicion in his tone.

"Fine. Everyone is fine. The little boys have missed you."

Just like a mother. Guilt him with the emotions of innocent children. "I've missed them too. I'll get in touch with Zach and Angus this week and arrange to take the boys out."

"That would be nice." She scooped another helping of eggs and added fruit onto his nearly empty plate. "But why don't you ask Nic to come to family dinner this weekend? I'd love to meet her. Well, you know, as your girlfriend meet her. Of course, I could always go down to the bakery, but I don't want her to think I'm trying to ambush her when she's concentrating on work. And you can tell her she doesn't even have to bring dessert."

"I can ask, but like I said, she doesn't like to leave her aunt alone to care for her mother too often. She may say no."

"Then do your best to make her say yes." She picked at her plate with her fork, all the while regarding him with a considering eye and a little smile playing on her lips. "Look at my baby becoming a man."

"Aw, Ma, you're starting in on the baby stuff again."

"I can't help myself. I'm so proud of you. Some men your age would look at a girl like Nic and the responsibilities she has and turn tail and run. But not you. You're in love, aren't you?"

There was no bother denying it. He had fallen in love with Nic from the moment she first turned those big brown eyes on him. When she truly smiled at him for the first time, those luscious lips sealed the deal.

"Yeah, yeah I am. She's amazing. Smart, funny, sexy as—" he cleared his throat—"She has a good personality."

His mother swatted him on the arm. "You can admit she's sexy. I'm not surprised she has talents in that area if she has your attention. You Maguire men are a randy lot."

"Mom!"

"What?" She blinked at him with innocence. "I've birthed six children. Don't go thinking for one second that your father and I have only had sex six times. Your father is a sex machine."

"That's it." He placed his hands over his ears. "I'm scarred for life now. You've broken me. And I'm going to have to tell all of my brothers what you just said so they can share my pain."

"Oh, stop it. Don't you see, Adam? I love your father, and he loves me. And even forty years later we have an active sex life, because we care for each other. That's what I want for you.

To find a girl that you would move mountains for to be by your side forever. And it sounds as if you have."

"I hope I have. Nic is a little more hesitant to put a label on our relationship. Hell, she's a *lot* more hesitant. I think I'm going to have to break her into the idea of forever real slow."

"You can do it. I know of at least ten girls who are in love with you already. If she isn't, she soon will be." She clasped her hands to her chest and heaved a happy sigh. "Oh, this is wonderful. Soon you'll be married and having children. You know, I'll get your father to contact Gerald at Valley Construction and have them start breaking ground on your house right away. That way you'll be all set to move in once you're married."

"Wait, wait. What? You lost me. What house?"

"Your house. The one we've been waiting to build for you on the ranch."

Ah, jeez. Leave it to his mother to go from zero to a hundred in a nanosecond. He could barely get Nic to agree they were remotely serious about each other, and here was his mother decorating a house that didn't even exist.

"Mom, back up a little. First, I need to get Nic to realize she can't live without me. Then we'll focus on where we'll set up house. More than likely it will be at the Fournier house, or close to town so she can be with her mother. And of course, I already have a home here."

"Here?" she exclaimed as if he announced he was from another planet. "Surely you're joking."

"Why? This is my home and where I work. We'd be happy here."

"Adam Patrick Maguire, you are being obstinate on purpose." She gestured to the room around them. "This is a bachelor pad. A stop on a cowboy's journey as he roams from ranch to ranch. This is not a house for a couple to live in. A couple looking to start a family. Unless…" She gasped and slapped her hands over her mouth as her eyes widened. She pulled her fingers away from her lips to whisper. "Unless you, and Rafe, and Jack are…sharing Nic, like Ben and Colby."

"What?" he exclaimed with a shout then bit his lip. "Geez, Ma, what has gotten into you today? No, I don't share my girlfriends. And what is so bad about living wherever you please?"

"I want you home," his mother stated, and shifted in her seat while pulling down the ends of her cardigan. "With the family."

"I *am* with family."

"These people are not your blood," she spat.

"No. They're the family *I* chose. But make no mistake, I love them just as much as I do Dad and my brothers. And you."

"But you're so far away."

"I'm only across town."

"Don't you get it?" she shouted as her eyes filled with tears. She reached out and grabbed his hand with both of hers, squeezing his fingers in a death lock. "It's too far away. I need you close. I need to see you every day. Kiss your head, and hear your voice, and know that you are safe. I need to know that you're not—like—Scott—"

The trickle of tears turned into a raging river as sobs shook her shoulders. In a heartbeat, he was up with his arms wrapped around her as she wept into his chest. He didn't utter a sound as they rocked back and forth, figuring it was best to have the rhythmic beat of his heart do the talking for him. Remind her he was still alive and well.

"I'm sorry." She hiccupped and patted his shirt where her tears had soaked through. "I just miss him so much."

"I miss him, too. He was my favorite brother. He never made me feel like I was an accident, or just his kid brother. He actually played with me."

"Oh, Adam." His mother drew back and laid her hand on his cheek. "All of your brothers love you."

"Love me, maybe. But they sure don't act like they *like* me. I'm more of a nuisance than anything."

"That's not true. They're just Maguires, and the Maguire men have a hard time showing their affections. Now, you and Scott always took more after my side of the family. It's probably why you two got along so well, and why I miss you both so terribly."

Adam sat back down in his chair, but took a hold of his mother by the hand. "Mom, I have no idea what to say to make you feel better. Life is unpredictable, you know that, and at times it sucks hard. Having me live on the Maguire ranch isn't a guarantee to keep me safe."

"I know. I know." She sniffled and looked at their joined hands. Suddenly she jerked her chin up with a gasp. "Is that why you'd rather work here? Did your brothers drive you away?"

"No," he shot back immediately, then sucked in a breath. Well... "Maybe. I wouldn't say they drove me away. I just wanted to be elsewhere. I didn't want to be the runt anymore, or referred to as only the little brother. Or the low man on the totem pole *all of the time*. I just want to be Adam. And here, I can be me. Just me."

"There is no 'just' you, sweet pea. You are so much more than just. You're a good boy. No. You're a good man."

"Thanks, Ma."

She reached for the roll of paper towels that sat on the table and ripped off a sheet to dab at her eyes. "But you'll always be my baby. Sorry, sweet pea."

"Well, being a mother's favorite son is a burden, but I'll take the lumps if I have to," he said with a suffering sigh. Then he flashed his mother a huge grin and a wink.

"Oh, you." She swatted his arm. "Now, tell me more about Nic and why you think she's your one and only."

"I will have to get to work at some point this morning."

"Then start talking, mister. And if your boss has a problem with that, he can take it up with me."

"All right, all right," he said, laughing.

Huh. Maybe he should set his mother after Nic to talk up his finer points. With luck, he'd have a ring on her finger by Christmas.

Chapter Nine

D ESPITE THE AIR conditioning being cranked to arctic-blast
level, Nic felt sweat gathering under her arms and over
her lip as she drove down the winding lane of the Sprawling A
Ranch.

Per Adam's instructions, she parked in front of the detached
garage across from the main house with the grand porch
wrapping around the front like a comforting shawl. A swing
hung from the rafters, loaded with pillows in a profusion of
colors. She bet the Armstrongs spent many nights rocking away
while watching the sunset. In her opinion, it would be a travesty
if they didn't.

Down the road she spotted the flutter of tablecloths on the
picnic tables that had been set out for the barbecue. Trey
Armstrong was working the grill, somehow managing to appear
unaffected by the summer sun as he stood between the massive
cooktop and nearby fire pit that was already blazing. A few of
the other ranch hands appeared, carrying ice chests and benches
to sit on, but Adam was nowhere to be seen.

She took a moment to check out her reflection in the visor
mirror and made a face at the sight of all the perspiration wetting
her brow.

"Good lord," she muttered and reached for the glove box to pull out a few napkins she had stored there from various fast food restaurants to blot away the sweat. Attractively dewy was passable. End of marathon drenched was not.

Why she was so nervous was beyond her. Most of Adam's friends she had met many times before, having either gone to school with them or as customers for the bakery. Heck, the summer before, she had been on the phone with Gabriella at least twice a week with wedding business. But her instincts were pinging at her, hardcore, that this party was not just another date. With her arrival at the ranch, her relationship with Adam was about to turn into something more serious than a few weeks of dating and fantastic sex.

Wasn't that a good thing? Wasn't that how it was supposed to work? Meet, go out, have sex, meet his friends, meet his family, and then...

And then.

Right.

It was the "and then" that freaked her out as if she were standing at the edge of a bungee platform with only a rubber band for the cord.

Sure, they had only been together for about six weeks, but she already felt closer to Adam than to any man she had ever been with. He was just so darn affectionate and supportive and wonderful. Even when he was acting his goofiest, he was adorable. And on top of that, he was a good man. Not too many of them in the world nowadays. She'd be a fool if she didn't hold on to him forever.

But he didn't belong to her. He belonged to Mission.

Adam was never going to leave that town. He loved it there, felt at one with the community who looked upon him as a favorite son.

There was nothing wrong with loving your hometown and wanting to make a life there, except Mission didn't hold the same appeal for her.

Mission was nothing but the same old, same old. Every. Single. Day.

What was the point of being alive if you didn't stretch your wings and try something new once in a while? In Mission, new was akin to weird, and weird was treated as something to be afraid of or ignored. That kind of life would crush her soul.

But Adam was entitled to his opinion, just as she was entitled to hers, which meant there was no way their futures could align.

So what was she doing, going to meet his friends? If she had any compassion for him, she'd back right out of the driveway and let him go with the wish for him to find a girl who was ready to be his other half of American Gothic.

Yeah, that's what she should do. End it now before she hurt him with her inability to tie her life to Mission.

A knock on the glass made her jump in her seat. "Hey, Nic. There you are."

Adam stood at the passenger door with the sun shining on him as if he were an angel. His cowboy hat was set at a rakish tilt on his head, and his smile was so wide, it almost hurt to look at him, he was so handsome.

Yep. She was a horrible, selfish person, she thought as she reached for the door handle. A horrible, selfish person who wanted to spend as much time as possible with the handsome cowboy who made her happy.

"Hi. Sorry I'm late. We had a last-minute rush with the boys from football camp. Those kids really like cookies."

"No problem. I'm just glad you're here and there wasn't any trouble at home."

"No trouble, just busy. Aunt Jacqui said if I didn't leave, she'd come in my place and send me pictures. She thinks I should leave the house more often."

"Your aunt is the best. Now come here." He drew her in close for a hello kiss that was so steamy, she wished his friends weren't a few dozen yards away. Seriously, the man made her consider fastening all of her clothes with Velcro for easy access.

But his friends *were* close by and watching them with great interest, she noticed as she pulled away and glanced in their direction.

"Where ya going, darlin'?" Adam asked and tried to swoop in for another lip lock.

"Later, cowboy. We have an audience."

"I say, let 'em watch."

"And I say, help me carry these desserts."

"Desserts?" The desire in his eyes changed from that for sex to that for sweets. "Ooo. What did ya bring?"

She reached into the backseat then handed him two pink boxes. "Cherry pie and a Samoa cheesecake."

"Cheesecake? *The* cheesecake? Sweetness, why are you sharing? That is something that is a secret best kept between the two of us."

"Well, that's not being friendly." She picked up a small cooler and shut the car door with her hip.

"I know these men. They will not appreciate your talents the way I do."

"So you're saying you're looking out for me and sparing me any heartache over being underappreciated?"

"You know me so well."

"I do." She smiled. "That's why we're sharing."

"Darn." He winked. "I thought I had you there."

A tall Hispanic man with the whitest teeth she had ever seen came up to them and reached for one of the boxes. "Here, let me help you with that, Maguire. Wow. It looks delicious."

"What, you have X-ray vision? You don't even know what it is," Adam said.

"It's from Dulce Vita. I know it's delicious." He turned to her and his smile widened. "Hi. I'm Rafe."

"Back away, Montoya," Adam warned with a narrow-eyed glare. "The only sweetness you're getting from my girl is her pastries."

"Calm down, young buck. I have no designs on your girl." Somehow his smile brightened. "Unless you become a dick and she wants to know what it's like to be with a real man."

"Rafe, knock it off," interjected a woman with similar dark hair and as gorgeous a smile as the flirty cowboy. "You're gonna give him an aneurysm. Hi, Nic. Please ignore my brother. He lives to pester."

"Hello, Gabriella. So this is the brother you've talked about?"

"Unfortunately, yes." Brother and sister made disgusted faces at each other, but Nic saw the love in their eyes as they did so. "Come on, let's get you something cool to drink."

"It all smells so wonderful," Nic exclaimed as they passed the picnic tables covered with bowls of fruit, baked beans, and potato salad.

Trey waved with a set of tongs in his hands. "Nothing beats the scent of sizzling cow."

"Ugh, you make that sound so appetizing," said a beautiful redhead as she placed a huge salad bowl on the table. "Salad is ready, and look," she held up both hands. "All of my fingers are intact, so stop it with the cooking jokes."

"Faith is a little challenged when it comes to the kitchen," Gabriella murmured to Nic. "But I love her too much to tell her making a salad isn't cooking."

Faith smiled, seemingly oblivious to the comment, and held out her hand. "Hi, Nic. Do you remember me from school? I was a year ahead of you."

"Yeah. You were in all of the school plays, right?"

"That was me. I remember you had the best collection of shoes. Still do, I see."

"Thanks."

"Quit hogging Nic and send her my way," Greta called out from her perch on a lounge chair. An oversized beach umbrella shielded her from the late afternoon sun and she had her feet submerged in the water held by the kiddie pool that was set up in front of her. "It's good to see you."

"Thank you for having me." She bent to give Greta a hug. Or at least tried to, but Greta's very pregnant belly prevented too much contact. "How much longer do you have to go?"

"Four weeks," replied everyone in the vicinity at once.

"Stop it," Greta scowled, even as she bit back a laugh. "I haven't been that bad. It's just so damn hot. Take it from me, Nic, do not have a baby in summer."

"Since I don't plan on having children, period, I don't think it will be an issue."

"Never?" Adam asked. "Like never ever?"

One would have thought she told him pizza caused impotency, judging by the shock in his eyes.

Kids were cute. As long as they weren't hers. So no, she didn't pine for the large house, picket fence, and two-point-five kids. She liked having as few responsibilities as possible and to be able to take off at a moment's notice if she wanted. Of course, those opportunities were long in the past now that she had her mother to take care of, which made her long for those occasions all the more.

But even she had to concede, the future was still undetermined. Opinions had the luxury of being changed, and weird things were wont to happen.

"Well, I'd never say never, but I doubt I'll ever have children. It's too hard to travel the world with a baby."

"So there is a possibility you still want them."

"I'm ninety-nine percent certain I won't."

He nodded with a smile. "I see. I see."

Oh, God. Now didn't that sound as if he was making plans for a future. With her. And babies.

The odds of her changing her mind about offspring were about one in a million-gazillion. However, she was now one hundred percent certain they were going to have to have a come-to-Jesus moment about the expectations each had about their relationship. This ambiguity could not continue.

"Nic, would you like a drink?" Gabriella held out a tall glass of lemonade. As she offered a second glass to Greta, she gestured with a nod into the distance and muttered, "Alert. Alert."

Greta's spine straightened. Her smile fell and her lips tightened into a thin line. "Ah, crap. Nic, why don't you sit by me and we can get to know each other better?"

A glance over Greta's shoulder gave Nic an idea about the sudden change in her demeanor.

Stacy Durante sauntered in their direction on platform sandals that added another three inches to her tall, lithe frame. A bubblegum-pink halter top and matching short-shorts revealed acres of golden skin that appeared several shades darker in comparison to her white-blonde hair. The woman was a walking, talking Barbie doll and just as plastic.

The entire Durante clan made Nic's stomach sour, and it was just her luck that she had to deal with all three sisters through school. In her opinion, Stacy's older sister Ronnie was the nastiest. But that could be because they had been in the same grade. Mission High was only so big, and Ronnie had been the queen bee, with her entourage of drones willing to carry out her catty wishes.

Still, Stacy most certainly carried the Durante genes and wore the "Who do you think you are, you insignificant twat?" expression like a pro. And if memory served Nic correctly, Adam's ex, Angela, was tight with the Durante sisters. Awesome.

"Is Stacy a friend of yours?" Nic asked.

"Jack's girlfriend," Greta replied with a pained smile. "She's real pretty."

She shrugged. "If you go for that."

"Jack goes for that. Lucky us," Gabriella clarified and her lips twisted as if she had sucked on a lemon before she waved in greeting. "Stacy, hi. How are you?"

"I'll be better once Jack gets me something cold to drink." The statuesque blonde smiled at them in turn until she spotted Nic and she grimaced as if she had stepped in cow manure. With a snarl of her lip she sneered, "Nicolette."

"Stacy. Fancy seeing you here."

"Yes," she drawled and her gaze narrowed. "What *are* you doing here?"

"Adam invited me."

"Adam?" Her blonde eyebrows jumped to her hairline. "Are you two still seeing each other? I thought that died down a long time ago. Hmm."

"Hmm. Yes." Nic copied her disgruntled hum and left it at that. If she were to be polite and try to engage her in conversation, chances were Stacy was either going to find a way to ridicule her, or heaven forbid, try to carry on an actual conversation.

Greta choked on a giggle. "Nic, I saw Adam carrying a pink

box. Did you bring something sinfully delicious?"

"Of course."

"Ugh," Stacy sighed. "More junk food? Really, I'm surprised the guys aren't fatter with the way you all feed them. And, Greta, a little baby weight is all right, but you're approaching whale status."

"Holy shit," Nic exclaimed while the other women gasped. "I can't believe you just insulted your hostess straight to her face."

Stacy waved a dismissive hand. "I did no such thing. I'm just concerned for Greta's health."

"Sure you are," Gabriella muttered. "Trey, give me those tongs and come take your wife's hand. She needs you."

"Magpie?" Trey asked and sprinted to her side once he saw her staring into the distance. "Greta, darlin', what's wrong? Is it the baby?"

"Tell her she's pretty," Gabriella said. "And don't skimp on the sentiment."

Stacy flounced away with all the obliviousness of her callous behavior usually reserved for reality television stars, while Nic and Faith left Trey some privacy to console his injured wife.

Gabriella hollered at them all to come and eat, and the ensuing scene reminded Nic of that old movie *Seven Brides for Seven Brothers* when the boys rolled into the kitchen like an avalanche and inhaled the feast Millie had worked all morning on. For a moment Nic was afraid fists would be thrown as Mark and Jack fought over a chicken leg.

"Don't wait too long, sweetness," Adam warned as he piled a chicken breast onto a stack of ribs. "This won't last long."

"Don't worry," Gabriella said in a hushed tone. "I kept a stash on the grill for us girls. That way we don't have to partake in this Lord of the Flies ritual."

"That's genius."

"Thank you," she said and saluted with the tongs.

As Nic filled her plate at a more sedate pace, she saw Gabriella take a plate of food over to Greta. Trey was on one knee at her side, pressing kisses to her cheeks as he glared over to where Stacy sat at a table with Jack, Colby, and Ben.

Gabriella held the plate out to Greta. "I saved the best steak for you."

"Oh." Greta blinked with long, slow bats of her lashes. "Thanks. But I'll just have a salad."

"What?" Gabriella shrilled, then lowered her voice. "You don't want a salad."

"Yes. I do. I'm not that hungry." She looked at her hands as she rubbed them over her belly.

Gabriella bent over until she was nose to nose with Greta. "If you are letting that princess wannabe stop you from having this steak that you have been looking forward to all day, I will take your baby and raise it as my own. You are pregnant and beautiful and she can go fuck off for all I care."

The line of Greta's lips wobbled before she broke out into a grin and reached for the plate. "Thank you. You're a good friend."

Trey threw his hands up. "I said those exact same things to you. Why do you believe Gabriella and not me?"

"Because you want to have sex with me. Well, at least you did. Maybe you never want to touch me again and are too nice to tell me," Greta ended on a sniffle.

"Do me a favor," he said to Gabriella as he took his wife in his arms. "Keep Stacy away from me. Forever."

"No problem." Gabriella turned and headed back to where Nic was standing.

Nic flashed her a big toothy grin and added a heaping

spoonful of potato salad to her plate in solidarity. There was no way she'd be able to eat that much food, but she could at least put on a good show.

Gabriella laughed. "I knew I liked you."

The two of them joined Adam, Mark, and Rafe.

"Sit yourself right here, Nic," Rafe said as he stood to allow her to slide onto the bench between him and Adam. "I cannot let the evening go by without complimenting you on your buns. They are the sweetest I've ever tasted."

"Montoya, I swear to God I will kick your ass," Adam growled.

"What?" He blinked, but innocence was far from his eyes that twinkled with devilish intent. "Nic is a genius with decadent delights. I'm just conveying my enjoyment of her treats."

"You are being evil is what you are," his sister interjected. "Knock it off."

Mark placed his hand over hers. "Now, honey, let 'em be. This is the most fun I've had around your brother. Ever."

Nic turned to Adam with a smile. "Aren't you glad you invited me?"

"Yes." He smacked a kiss on her lips. "Now you see how I suffer at the hands of my employers and can make it all better when we're alone."

Rafe and Mark made gagging sounds as Gabriella laughed. The mutual teasing only grew in ridiculousness as the cowboys continued to berate each other as if they were obnoxious brothers. But it was obvious by the light in their eyes that they all held a love and respect for each other that was just as strong as blood ties.

Except for that bit of unpleasantness with Stacy, the entire afternoon was some of the most fun Nic had had in way too long of a time.

They ate. They joked. Contests of skills were declared from horseshoe tossing to lassoing. When the guys took turns roping a metal steer, Nic cheered and made bets with the other girls over which cowboy could make the trickier shot. It looked as if Adam had the competition in the bag until Ben connected with a thirty-foot throw while sailing by on his horse at full gallop.

"No fair," Adam grumbled by her side. "He's kinky. You know he can rope anything with his eyes closed."

The beverage she was drinking tried to go down into her lungs as she sputtered. "Yeah. I had heard something about that."

He sidled closer and looped his arm around her shoulders. "You know, if you want to spice things up, I'm all for a little ropin'. But I draw the line at multiple partners. I don't want to share you."

When he looked at her as if he were already licking her from head to toe, she didn't want to be shared either. "I'll keep that in mind."

The kiss he planted on her was as hot as a profiterole pulled straight from the oven and dipped in molten caramel.

"Delicious," he said with a lick of his lips as he pulled away. "You taste like lemonade."

"And you taste like barbecue sauce."

"I'd like to smother you in barbecue sauce." He gripped her by the hips and hauled her into the curve of his body. "Actually, I'd like to smother you in a whole lot of things."

The surprise she had planned for later that evening burned her tongue with the need to be spilled, but she kept her lips together and hugged him tight.

"Are you having a good time?" he whispered in her ear and smoothed the palm of his hand down the full length of her hair.

She hummed and nodded. "Your friends are pretty cool."

It wasn't until he sagged in her embrace and sighed as if relieved did she realize he had been nervous about the meeting.

"What?" She drew back to cup his face in her hands. "Did you think I wasn't going to like them? Or they wouldn't like me?"

"I knew they'd love you, if they didn't already. But you, I wasn't so sure. You keep so much of what you're thinking locked inside, I never know where the wind is going to blow."

"Well, I like your friends. A lot." She glanced over his shoulder to where a certain blonde sprawled in a lounge chair as if she hadn't a clue, or even a care, as to what was going on around her. "However, I do question Jack's choice in women."

"Stacy? Aw, she's all right. Although she does tend to rub people the wrong way."

"That's putting it mildly. Let's just say I have a history with the entire family that I'd like to leave in the past."

"Oh." The light in his eyes faded and the corner of his lips turned down. He cuddled her closer, but this time his hug felt as if he were trying to protect her rather than the seductive embrace from only a moment before. "I understand."

Did he? Did he really? Did she even want him to understand the struggle of having to face a bully a decade after the fact?

Adam led a charmed life. To fault him for not having an inkling of what she had faced as a child was petty and plain stupid. The fact that he was trying to empathize with her now showed just how awesome of a guy he was.

For the rest of the evening, Adam was rarely more than an arm's length away, holding her hand, rubbing her back, or cuddling her close. By no means was he annoying, just attentive to her needs, more so than usual.

After the sun went down, they all gathered around the bonfire, roasting marshmallows and singing along with Ben as he played the guitar. As much as she disliked Mission, on a night like this with clear skies, friendly people, and a handsome cowboy whispering sweet nothings in her ear, it was all too easy to imagine many more nights spent the same way.

When her butt grew numb from sitting on the log for too long, she stood and dusted the seat of her pants off. Adam joined her and took her by the hand.

"Let's say you and me blow this pop stand and head back to my place?" He added a wiggle of his brow to his leering grin.

"Sounds fantastic. Let me grab a few things from my car."

"Just drive it on down the lane to the house. It'll be faster." He trailed a line of kisses down her neck, causing her to hang on to his shoulders as her knees gave out. "I'm growing impatient."

"I hope that's not the only thing growing."

"You are so bad. I love it." He laughed then smacked her on the ass. "Let's go."

"Good night," she said to Greta and Trey as they passed. "Thanks for the hospitality."

Greta lifted her arms. "Don't think you're leaving without giving me a hug. I'm so glad you came. I hope we'll see you again."

"You will," Adam answered. "I'll make sure of it."

After another round of good-byes, Adam held out his hand. "Shall we, my dear? Paradise awaits."

Chapter Ten

THE DRIVE TO the house Adam shared with Jack and Rafe took only a few seconds. Before she hit the brakes, he was out and collecting her overnight bag and a small cooler to bring into the house.

"What's in here?" he asked, indicating the blue Igloo.

"A surprise."

His eyes flashed with delight. "A sweet surprise?"

"I like to think so."

"Hot damn." He hustled her into his room so fast she didn't even have a chance to see much of the bachelor pad beyond the worn couches and monster television in the living room.

He set her things on the floor and reached for the top of the cooler. "My plan was to strip you naked the second I got you in here, but now I'm curious about what you brought."

"Don't touch." She smacked his hands. "Let me show you my way."

"I'm liking this already. Where do you want me?"

"On the bed."

"This keeps getting better and better." He leapt onto the bed with a bounce and lay back with his hands behind his head.

"Boots off, mister. I'm not fighting with those things."

While he shucked off his boots, she took a moment to survey his domain.

Nic couldn't remember the last time she was in a bedroom that was set up for only sleeping and other bed-related shenanigans. There wasn't a desk or a computer taking up real estate. No television was mounted on a wall, or anywhere else, for that matter. The bed was made, all of the laundry was tucked into the hamper, and a girlie calendar on the wall was censored with a strip of duct tape across the model's naked breasts.

"What is it with guys and the Three Stooges?" she asked, gesturing to the trio of posters covering the closet door. "I thought they only appealed to men in their sixties."

"Are you kidding? They're an American institution. Comedic geniuses."

"They're weird."

"Girls don't get it. They never get it." He sat up in alarm. "Is that a deal breaker between us? I'd hate to have to end things because you don't like my love of the Stooges."

"If our relationship ends over the Three Stooges, there are bigger issues at hand. Now, do you have a radio or docking station?"

"Over on the dresser."

In seconds, the woeful licks of Jimmie Page's guitar filled the room and Nic lost herself to the bluesy beat. She swayed back and forth as her hands drifted over her breasts and down her sides. A glance over her shoulder found Adam staring at her with his mouth hanging open and his breath escalating with each measure of music.

"Do you like?" she asked and slowly slid her T-shirt up and over her head, revealing a sheer, lacy red bra.

His Adam's apple bobbed. "I like. A lot."

She rolled her hips, shimmied her shoulders, and danced

closer to the foot of the bed, never taking her gaze off him as she reached for the clasp of her jeans.

"You're killing me, babe." His voice rumbled in his chest. She loved the way his cheeks grew pink and eyes flashed like sapphires. "Take it off now."

"So impatient." She bent over with her backside facing him and peeled the denim down her legs. By the time she revealed her matching red panties, she was certain he was going to come off the bed and rip her clothes off her.

She climbed onto the mattress and crawled between his legs. Trapped beneath the tight confines of his jeans was the hard length of his cock. Lowering her head, she puffed a stream of hot air against the fabric, delighting in his quick intake of breath. After a few passes, she leaned in and scraped her teeth over the ridge, testing his limits as she increased the pressure of her bites.

His hands landed on her head and she pulled away with a shake of her head. "Uh-uh. No touching. I want to play with you as I see fit."

"No, you want to kill me," he groaned. "I want your hot mouth on my naked skin."

"Like this?" she licked a trail up the inside of his arm.

"That works too. But you know what I mean."

She straddled his waist and encouraged him to sit up, tugging at the snaps of his shirt. Beneath the western-cut blue and green plaid gleamed a bright white tank top.

"Ugh." She pulled at his garments. "You wear too many clothes."

"I can say the same about you." He laughed and reached for the strap of her bra. "Get naked."

"In due time. And I said don't touch."

She pushed him back down and looked her fill at the lean, mean, hunk of man splayed out before her. With the tips of her fingers, she explored the contours of his chest, flicking at the nubs of his nipples and scoring soft pink lines down his sides. She loved the way his lashes fluttered and his mouth parted as she ground her hot mound against his erection. Although she told him not to touch, that didn't stop him from bucking his hips, striving for maximum contact.

A three-inch scar running across his rib cage that had always caught her eye beckoned for attention. She bent to lick along the dark line. "How did this happen?"

"Barbed wire."

She copied the movement on another scar over his shoulder. "And this one?"

"Barbed wire. It's dangerous stuff."

"I see. What about his one?" She flicked at a starburst-shaped mark on his biceps.

"Andrew shot a nail gun at me when I was fifteen. He didn't know it was on."

She sat up with a start. "He *shot* you with a nail gun?"

"Yep." A wide smile spread across his lips. "Mom got him good. Actually made him go out and cut a switch and spanked him with it."

"I would have shot him back with the nail gun."

"That's my little hellcat."

"Poor baby with such mean brothers. You're going to need lots of kisses."

"Oh yeah." His brows lowered and his smile turned into a pitiful frown. "Lots and lots of kisses. And sex. A lot of sex."

"We'll have to get more naked for that."

"That's what I've been saying," he shouted, throwing his hands in the air.

"But I like teasing you so much better."

She scooted down his legs until her mouth hovered over his

belly button. For the next fifteen minutes she delighted in making him gasp and writhe as she licked a path back and forth underneath the band of his jeans. When his whimpers turned into pleas, she finally took pity on him and set to work on removing the rest of his clothes. When the hot length of his cock burst from its confines as if surfacing from a deep dive, she let loose with a peal of giggles.

"That feels so much better," he said, sighing, and reached for his shaft.

"Hands to your side, mister. Or you won't get your treat."

"Nic, I swear to God, I'm about to go full bore on you."

"All right, all right." She jumped off the bed and retrieved the cooler she had set by the door.

If she could, she'd make a GIF of the way he looked just then with his body taut with sexual frustration and his nostrils flared like a bull in heat. If ever she had doubt as to her sex appeal, she'd only have to look at those few seconds of video to put a swish back into her swagger.

She withdrew a container from the cooler and opened the lid, revealing the creamy, dreamy dessert inside. "Voila!"

"Are you kidding me?" he screeched. "You want me to choose between sex and cheesecake? You are evil."

"Nope." She popped the release of her bra and slid out of the garment, allowing it to drop to the floor. "This is all about having sex *and* cheesecake."

The confection was not too warm or too cool against her finger as she scooped up a dollop and smeared the cream across her nipple. Straddling his hips, she leaned forward until the tip of her breast brushed his lips.

"I take it back," he said. "You're not evil. You're a genius."

The container in her hand almost took a tumble as he sucked her sweetened nipple into the cavern of his mouth with a voracious growl. With her other hand covered in cake, she only had the strength of her thighs to keep her upright. And with the way he licked and sucked at her flesh, she was ready to melt against him like a snow cone in an inferno.

Clouds of cotton candy swirled in her mind, tempting her away from her plan to be the dominant one in this scenario. The electric sensation of his callused palms dipping between her backside and her panties brought her back to her senses even as her body was more than willing to have him take over.

"My turn," she said with a gasp, as she pulled away from his talented mouth.

She painted his chest in strips of cream and raspberry sauce that she followed with her tongue and nips of her teeth. Down, down, she licked until she faced the throbbing length of his cock. This time she gathered a nice palm full of cheesecake and wrapped her hand around his shaft and pulled with a gentle tug.

Adam's hips shot off the bed. As she took her treat deep into her mouth, he cried out, his hands fisting into her hair as she bobbed up and down. Soon, the saltiness of his precum mixed with the sweetness of the dessert, creating a delicious morsel of goodness she wanted to gobble whole. Against her tongue, his cock hardened with his impending release.

"Where do you want to come, baby?" she asked, never once breaking the rhythmic stroking of her hand.

"Everywhere," he moaned. "Oh, God. That's so good, babe. I can't think straight."

"Mouth it is, then."

"No." He pulled on her hair. "In your pussy. I want to come in your pussy. Ride me, sweetness. I want you to ride me."

He didn't have to tell her twice. She jumped off the bed. "Where are the condoms?"

"Uh." He blinked several times and shook his head as if he

were trying to focus. "Nightstand."

The top drawer of his nightstand held an amusing assortment of prophylactics ranging from the plain vanilla sort to vanilla flavored.

"Hello, handsome," she chuckled and reached for a purple packet labeled as ribbed for her pleasure.

"Do we have to?" Adam panted as she crawled up between his legs and rolled the condom down his shaft.

"Do we have to what?"

"Use a condom. Why can't we go without?"

She froze, hovering with the tip of his cock poised at the entrance of her body. "Um, there's that whole pregnancy thing I'm trying to avoid."

"Is that all?" He slid his hands up and down her thighs. "Would getting pregnant really be so bad? Or do you just not want to have babies with me?"

Was he *insane?*

Judging by the hopeful light in his baby blues and the way he thrust his hips against her as if to say, come on, let's give it a go, she knew he was dead serious. Adam Maguire wanted to procreate. With her.

A fissure of resentment burned across her face and made her teeth clench.

Oh, sure. She should just put her life on hold to birth his offspring because he said so. Share her body with the fruit of his loins because it was something he wanted. And then be a mother to said child until their adulthood and beyond while Adam did who knew what in the meantime.

And those were just a few of the thousand and one reasons why his questions were the most ridiculous and misogynistic thing he had ever said to her.

For half a second she considered punching him in the balls

and telling him to go fuck himself and have his own babies.

But she didn't.

She didn't say a word. Didn't utter a single sound as she shifted her hips and slowly impaled herself on his latex-covered shaft.

Now who was the insane one?

Maybe they both were. Because while the idea of her becoming a mother was absolutely ludicrous, the idea of Adam being a father wasn't.

If the way he interacted with his nephews when he brought them into the bakeshop indicated how he'd be as a father, Adam was destined to be one of the greatest. He'd be one of those fathers who'd attend every sporting event, read bedtime stories at night, teach his children how to catch frogs or drive a tractor, and love their child to the point the kid would run away screaming, "Too much love. Too much love."

The woman who'd bear Adam's children would be lucky indeed. But that woman wasn't her. And for reasons she'd refused to name, that truth was like a serrated knife to the heart.

The pain of what wasn't meant to be raged like an out of control wildfire in her chest and brought tears to her eyes. Her jaw ached from clenching her teeth against a cry of sorrow as she worked her hips up and down, digging her nails into his shoulders as she tried to out-race her wayward thoughts.

Pleasure. She had to focus on the pleasure of his touch, the sound of his ragged moans, the friction of his body within hers. Images of a future spent apart were not wanted and were only tempting her to do something foolish, like rip the condom off and take the risk of being tied to him forever.

"You are so sexy," Adam groaned beneath her, stroking her with his hands in random patterns from her shoulders to her hips. "You're a freakin' goddess."

"Damn straight."

She wedged her hand between them and began to tug on her clit. Every inch of her body was aflame, but it wasn't enough. She needed it hotter, brighter. She needed to have her mind explode until she was numb to everything but the feel of Adam against her.

"That's it, baby," he gritted and bucked his hips harder and faster. "You're squeezing me so tight."

"More," she panted past dry lips. "More."

His eyes rolled back and he let loose a bellow she felt vibrate against her palms. As his orgasm ripped through his body, he never once stopped thrusting, driving into her again and again as he moaned, "Fuck, Nic."

Yes. Yes. Almost.

The supernova was so close, electrical pulses skipped over her skin. The frantic beats grew in intensity and size until they consumed her in its glorious light then detonated, exploding like the Death Star hit by a proton cannon.

And just as quick, all of that energy sucked back in, knocking the air from her lungs and leaving her a shaking mass on his chest.

"Aw, darling." He ran the tips of his fingers back and forth along her shoulders. "Every time with you gets better and better."

"Uh-huh," she replied, surprised she was even able to form a sound that was remotely articulate.

"Nic." He cupped her cheek in his hand and tilted her chin up to meet his gaze. His eyes were so dreamy, they hit her like a sucker punch to the gut. "Nic, I—I…"

Nothing else existed at that moment but Adam and the emotion swirling in his eyes. It was all laid out for her to see. The tenderness. The affection. And dare she name it—love. Yes, love was right there shimmering in his oh-so blue eyes, with an intensity that robbed her of her last remaining functioning brain cell.

And then he blinked and it was gone.

He cleared his throat and shifted. "I'm…going to get a towel. We're pretty sticky. But it was totally worth it."

Although he softened his withdrawal with a wink, Nic had never felt a loss so deep as the chill that rapidly seeped into her bones that not even the residual heat of his body on the bed sheets could hold at bay.

Maybe she was reading too much in his glance, but she sensed a wall had sprung up between them just then and she was the cause. All of the times she'd brushed off his exclamations of affection as being silly or too soon appeared to have finally taken root.

That's what she wanted, right? Nice and easy. No promises beyond that of a good time. No talk of forever, or babies, or love…

Love.

There was that word again. Again? Ha. As if it ever went away. She could delude herself all she wanted, but the truth was becoming harder to ignore. She was in love with Adam Maguire.

She buried her face into his pillow and muttered, "Well, shit."

"Are you okay?" he asked as he entered the room.

"Fine," came her muffled reply. She lifted up enough to offer him a smile. "I'm deliciously achy."

"You're just plain delicious." He popped her on the butt cheek and climbed onto the bed beside her with a damp towel in his hands. "Let me wipe you down."

Each stroke of his hands was heaven and hell. Never had she felt more cared for, but guilt over not being able to show him the affection he wanted burned a hole in her heart.

Even though she loved him, building a white picket fence–

type life in Mission was not in her future. To make him think otherwise was just cruel. The hourglass on their relationship as it currently stood held only so many grains of sand. How long could they maintain the status quo?

"Why the frown?" he asked, rubbing his thumb across her furrowed brow.

"Oh. Just wishing we had another piece of cheesecake." She forced a smile to her lips. "That was fun."

"It certainly was. And I am still hungry, but I'm in the mood for something different." His eyes sparkled with mischief as he slid his palm up the inside of her thigh and cupped her mound. "Something more like pie."

"You are such a dork," she said, snorting with laughter.

"Yeah, but you lov—like it."

Before she had realized she moved, she had reached out and held his face between her hands. Indecision over confessing how she felt about him or ignoring his stutter altogether made her teeth clench and her lips pinch together.

A few deep breaths passed as they stared into each other's eyes before she relaxed her fingers against his cheeks. "I do."

Disappointment flashed across his face for a heartbeat before he leaned down and took her lips in a kiss that spoke of his frustration.

She was a coward. A grade-A coward who should walk away from him that moment and let him find his forever.

But of course, she stayed exactly where she was and allowed him to roll her beneath the hot weight of his body as his hands spoke of the words she wouldn't allow.

Okay, she was a coward *and* selfish.

Well, in the words of another selfish and cowardly woman, tomorrow was another day. Their come-to-Jesus moment was going to have to wait.

Chapter Eleven

"YOU CAN DO this," Nic mumbled as she stepped out of the shower and ran a towel over her body. "It's not as if you're breaking up. Just clarifying expectations. That's all. Yeah. You can do this."

She *had* to do this. Guilt had weighed on her mind like a fifty-pound sack of flour and kept her awake while Adam slept beside her as if all was right in the world. His soft snores never faltered, and she would know. She watched him all night long, wondering if that was to be their last night together and loath to miss one second.

Best-case scenario was their relationship wouldn't change a bit. But who knew what Pandora's box of mayhem would unleash when a dialogue began and emotions were brought into the mix. Possibilities abounded, ranging from *All's well* to *It's over, sweetheart.*

It was that uncertainty that drove her from Adam's warm, cozy bed to the cold shower where she hoped to find fresh perspective. If one was going to confront her boyfriend with a potentially relationship ending topic, it would be a lot easier to do when not carrying his manly scent on one's skin. As it was, she might have to close her eyes the entire time to avoid looking at his handsome face. Too many times she had fallen prey to his puppy dog expression when he wanted to get his way.

Well, not this time. As soon as he wiped the sleep from his eyes, they were going to get down to the nitty-gritty.

"What the—?" she muttered and sorted through her clothes again and again.

Shirt, bra, jeans. Where the hell were her panties?

"Ugh." She heaved a sigh and tucked the towel as best she could under her arms.

Holding her clothes against her chest with one arm, she gripped the towel where the sides barely touched, and opened the door with her free hand.

"Well, well, well. What do we have here?"

Oh, fuck. Come on. Seriously?

Of all the people to run into while naked, it would have to be Eastern Washington Barbie blocking her path. Dressed in a cream-colored bra and panty set and nothing else, Stacy looked like the models who graced many a teenage boy's bedroom wall, and some adult boys, too.

Stacy flipped her sex-tousled hair over her shoulder and placed her hands on her hips in what Nic was sure was a well-practiced pose. "I thought I heard a pig squealing last night. Should have known it was you."

It was so tempting to drop everything and rush the bitch with fists flying, clothes or no clothes, but Nic was just insecure enough to clutch the towel tight to her chest. Besides, verbal altercations were more her style.

"Really?" Nic asked as she arched her brow. "That's all you got?"

Stacy's lashes fluttered as she shifted her weight. "I don't understand."

"Of course you don't, honey. Let me explain. That was a

lame insult, not to mention juvenile. But when the only reason you passed high school was because your mother was the principal's little piece on the side, I guess that's to be expected. Better luck next time."

Stacy cut her off as she tried to pass. "Adam may be slumming it with you now, but we all know you're nothing but white trash. Before you know it, he'll be back with Angela, and we'll all be laughing at how you thought you two actually had a future together."

"Adam is free to be with whomever he wants, and if we part ways, then we part ways. But what strikes me as funny is that you think I actually care about your opinion. Newsflash: I don't. I don't give a shit about you, or your friends, or anything in this two-bit town. I'm just passing through. So you just go on and fester away in your little do-nothing world. While you and your friends are spending yet another night down at The Crescent with your moonshine, I will be partying it up in New York, or drinking whiskey on a moor in Scotland, or bathing in champagne in France. But never will I spend one second thinking, 'Gee, I wish I'd tried harder to be friends with that raving bitch Stacy. My life just isn't as fulfilling as it could be.'"

"You better watch yourself, Nicolette." Stacy's nostrils flared as a red flush raced up her neck. "With one word I can destroy you, your business, and have your loony mother put away for good."

Nic tightened her grip on the towel to resist forming a fist and messing up Stacy's nose job.

"Wow." It was a battle keeping the rage in her voice in check. "The level of your delusion is staggering. You don't have as much pull in this town as you think you do, Stacy. As a town councilman, your father may, on a good day, but you have none. Nada. And my mother may be crazy, but she's not bat-shit psychotic like you."

"I'm not done with you," Stacy shouted as Nic tried again to pass. She reached out and pulled Nic by the hair.

"Ow," Nic cried out. "What the fuck are you doing?"

"No one disrespects me. No one," Stacy shrieked.

The door to Jack's room flew open. He rushed through all bare-chested with his unbuttoned jeans barely staying on his hips. "Stacy. Goddamn, girl, what are you doing?"

Just as quick as Stacy latched on, she let go, causing Nic to stumble into the wall.

"It's just a little girl talk." Stacy strode to Jack's side and cuddled against him as if she hadn't just assaulted Nic. "Nicolette and I were having a difference of opinion."

Nic didn't bother to wait to hear Jack's response. She ran for Adam's room and almost knocked him over as she burst through the door with so much force, it hit the wall and slammed shut on its own.

"Nic. What's going on?"

"Nothing."

Out in the hall, Jack and Stacy's voices grew louder as Nic's face grew hot. It was one thing to have to deal with Stacy's stupidity, but another altogether to have Jack witness the encounter. Who knew how much of her naked ass he saw in the struggle.

Adam gestured to the door. "That didn't sound like nothing. What happened?"

"None of your concern."

Heat continued to consume her, and the walls closed in. Unless she got out of the house immediately, she was going to go Hulk on the place.

She dropped the towel and her clothes on the floor, then dressed in only the essentials. Screw undergarments. At this point she only needed to be covered enough to get in the car and drive home.

"Nic, you're scaring me. What is going on?"

"Stacy is just being her normal, bitchy self." She tossed the rest of her clothes and her makeup bag in her duffle. "Look, I gotta go. I'll talk to you later."

"Nic. Wait."

There was no waiting. There was no any of anything as all sound muted into a dull roar and her vision narrowed to a thin strip of the few feet before her as she ran to the front door and down the stairs to her car. A cloud of dust rose as she hit the gas hard and the tires squealed until they caught traction and took off like a rocket.

That wasn't the first time someone tried to make her feel less than. And if she stayed in Mission, she'd bet the bakery it wasn't going to be the last. But the Stacys of the world best be on high alert if they thought she was going to stand there and take it. If Jack hadn't appeared when he did, naked or not, she would have taken Stacy to the floor and torn her extensions out, one by one. Justified? Yes. Respectable? Absolutely not.

"Fuck." She hit the steering wheel once, then again. Wasn't stupid high school shit supposed to end with graduation?

Yeah, right. Who was she kidding? The scars of youth were just that, scars. Perhaps they faded with time, but they were with you for life. What she was supposed to be long past with was allowing people to get under her skin.

She was a calmer soul now. More mature. Able to stop a tirade with an arch of her brow. No one ruffled her feathers. No one. Especially not stupid bitches from Mission, Washington.

Paris was nine hours ahead. Right at that moment she could be sitting outside a little patisserie, sipping café au lait and eating macarons until she exploded. Or she could be in England, watching Manchester United on a telly in a pub with a pint and a basket of chips. Or she could be in New York having brunch at the Neue Museum with Megan, eating overpriced pancakes and picking out which Broadway show they wanted to see.

Megan… If there was ever a time for some girl talk, it was now.

She reached for her cell and hit the speakerphone.

"What up, girlfriend?" Megan's familiar soprano sang across the line. Nic had long ago lost count of the number of times Megan got in a fight when someone made fun of her voice that sounded as if she had just sucked in helium. Some found the squeak grating, but to Nic, it was home.

"The sun," Nic replied.

"Hey, yeah. It's early there. What's going on? Is your mother okay?"

"Fine. Everyone's fine. I need you to tell me about what's going on in your world right this second. Every little insignificant detail."

"As in this second, this second? Gosh." She huffed out a breath. "Michael is trying to fix the A/C that crapped out last night, and it's hotter than hell out. Seriously, humidity can suck my dick. If he can't get it going soon, I'm heading to the spa and spending all day there. He can stay with the girl, who is insane. Nic Jr. is in a time out because she gave the dog a haircut worthy of Edward Scissorhands. And we have new neighbors from India, which means they cook curry *all, of, the, time*. I love Indian food, but I don't want to smell it twenty-four hours a day. Between that and the heat, my morning sickness is out of control."

"It sounds wonderful," she said when Megan paused for a breath.

"What? Oh, honey. If that is not a cry for help, I don't know what is. Michael," she shouted away from the speaker. "Nic is in trouble. I'll be in the bedroom. Don't bother me unless someone is bleeding.

There were a few rustles and the sound of a door clicking closed before Megan was back on the line. "Start at the beginning. What's his name?"

Nic chuckled. "I never said anything was wrong. Nor did I mention a man."

"You didn't need to. I can hear it in your voice. So spill it, sister, or I'm flying out there on my broomstick."

"Give me a second."

Nic turned onto a dirt road that ran between two fields of asparagus and turned off the engine as she reached above her head to open the sunroof. Reclining her seat all the way back, she settled into place, gazing up at the fluffy white clouds, and sighed into the phone. "His name is Adam. And I'm going to break his heart."

☆   ☆   ☆

"NIC!" ADAM SHOUTED from the front porch dressed only in his boxer shorts. He waved his hands in front of his face to clear the dust that exploded from beneath the rear tires of her car as she tore off down the lane. Confusion and worry hit him as if a calf had run right into his gut. Dragging a hand over his stubbled chin, he stomped back into the house, where Jack and Stacey were going out it like rabid mountain lions.

"Why did Nic run out of here like her ass was on fire?" he shouted.

"Ask *her*," Jack gritted out between his teeth and nodded at his girlfriend. He stood with his feet apart and his arms folded across his chest. His nostrils flared as a slash of red colored his cheeks.

Adam rounded on Stacy. "What did you do?"

She turned her astonished gaze toward him before copying Jack and crossing her arms under her breasts, pushing them up to create a shelf. She shrugged. "Why must you think *I* did something? She's the one who came in here with an attitude."

Not the right answer. "*What did you do?*"

Standing before two obviously pissed-off cowboys, Stacy lost her bravado and began to tremble. "I just reminded Nic where her place was," she admitted in a sulky tone.

"She attacked her," Jack answered.

"I did no such thing," Stacy gasped as Adam shouted with a surprised, "What?"

"That's what it looked like to me," Jack said. "When I came out here, Stacy was pulling Nic's hair. And they were arguing."

For the first time in his life, Adam lost his cool and advanced on the woman. "Who the fuck do you think you are? What did Nic ever do to you?"

Stacy let out a squeak as she backed into the wall. "Why are you yelling at me? I did you a favor. We all know she doesn't belong. She's weird. Angela is the girl for you. Hell, anyone else is the girl for you but that tramp."

"Nic is a whole lot classier than you," Jack said before Adam could finish drawing in an outraged breath. "God. I can't believe I'm such an idiot. Just—just get your things and go. I don't want to see you anymore."

Her lashes fluttered as her jaw dropped. "Are you breaking up with me?"

"Yeah. I am."

Her gaze jumped wildly between the two men, neither of whom batted an eye. When it became obvious nothing more was going to be said, an icy cool demeanor settled over her features, drawing her lips into a tight line. She laid her hand on her lace-clad hip and sashayed toward Jack.

"Well. If that don't beat all. You know, the reputation of the Sprawling A is going downhill every day. Pretty soon, no one in town will have anything to do with you. You better watch yourself, boys." She turned on her manicured foot and said over her shoulder, "You'll regret this, Jack Cannon. I'm the best thing that'll ever happen to you."

"I doubt that, darling," he drawled. "But whatever helps you sleep at night."

With a harrumph, she slammed the bedroom door shut. Once the sound stopped reverberating in his ears, Adam turned toward Jack.

"I'm sorry," they said in unison.

"No." A humorless chuckle passed Jack's lips. "I'm sorry I brought *that* into the house."

"And I'm sorry Stacy wasn't up to snuff." Adam rubbed the back of his neck and shook his head. "Did all of this really go down?"

"Yeah. It was the strangest thing I ever saw. So Nic took off, huh?"

"Yep. Oh, shit." He raced to his room and searched for his cell, punching the button for Nic.

"*Bonjour,* this is Nic. Leave a message."

"Nic. It's Adam. Please come back and talk to me. Call me right away."

He tried the number again and cursed when it went straight to voice mail.

"Damn." He tossed the phone onto the rumpled bed that still held the scent of her skin then reached for his jeans.

The door to Jack's room flew open and Stacy marched out with her nose raised high in the air. A few white feathers stuck to her hair and danced behind her as she strode out the front door.

"Damn," Jack muttered and scratched his jaw, surveying his room. "Looks like I'm gonna have to take a trip into the city to get new bedding."

"Tore it up, huh?" Adam asked.

"Enough. Man, she even ripped the arms off my GI Joes."

"Which ones?"

"All of them."

"Oh, that's harsh. No woman has a right to destroy a man's anything. Especially his Joes."

"Have you gotten hold of Nic yet?" Jack asked, his voice muffled from somewhere in his room.

"No." He put the phone on speaker and kept hitting redial. "I'm heading down to her house now. Can you let Trey know where I've gone?"

Jack met him in the hallway. "I'll go with you."

"You don't have to, man."

"I want to." A haunted look stole into his eyes that Adam hadn't seen since Gabriella's ex-husband and his cronies beat the crap out of him. "I want to make sure she's okay."

"I hear ya. Come on. Let's go."

Chapter Twelve

N IC WASN'T ALL that surprised to see Adam's truck parked
outside of her house. As usual, her phone call with Megan
had lasted several hours. Only her need to pee and her unwill-
ingness to do so in the middle of a field of asparagus ended their
conversation.

The more than a dozen missed messages he had left tickled
her conscience. She knew she should have called him back right
away, but she needed space. Part of her hoped he was so busy
with his ranch work, she'd have the entire day to put the
morning behind her. Then there was the other part, the more
selfish part, that was glad to see him there despite her radio
silence.

She turned the knob of the front door and pushed it open
just enough to peek inside to get a bearing as to where her aunt
and her mother might be entertaining their guest.

"There she is," her mother exclaimed.

Damn. She was going to have to turn in her stealth card.

Adam sat at what had become his place at the corner of the
couch. But it was the man seated next to him that stopped her at
the door in surprise.

"Hey, Nic," Jack said as he rose to his feet. "I'd like to talk to you for a minute."

"Umm… Sure. I guess," she replied and took a step back onto the porch.

Jack joined her and shut the door behind him. For several moments they stood in silence as he twirled his hat in his hands with a frown etched on his brow.

"I'm sorry," he finally said. "About Stacy. And I want you to know I broke up with her. She won't be by the ranch anymore. So you don't have to worry about seeing her again."

"You broke up with her because of me?"

"Mostly. I kind of suspected she behaved differently when I wasn't around. But by me burying my head in the sand, that put you in danger. And I'm sorry."

"I wouldn't say I was in danger. Stacy was looking to get her clock cleaned any second."

A small smile curled the corner of his mouth. "By you and me both, sister."

She bit her lip and gathered the courage to be bold to get personal. "Can I ask you a question?"

"Sure."

"Why were you going out with her?"

Surprise flashed in his eyes before he let out a huge sigh and rubbed at his jaw, suddenly finding the floor of the porch very interesting.

"You don't have to answer."

"No. No. It's a valid question. I just don't think I care for the answer. I would like to say it was her sparkling personality that attracted me, but truth? She's hot." His hand drifted to his nose where he rubbed his forefinger over where it had appeared to be recently broken. "With gossip the way it is in this town, you probably heard about when Gabriella's ex jumped me outside The Crescent. Well, it left me in bad shape for a while.

And to have a pretty girl pay attention to me, well..." A red flush raced up his neck. "Yeah, I let my dick rule my head."

"Well, at least you're man enough to admit it. That speaks a lot about your character. Thanks for the apology, Jack. I appreciate it."

"So we're friends?"

"Yes. We're friends."

He let out a breath and a sly grin stole across his lips. Jack the charmer was back in full effect. He gestured toward the front door. "Now, my best friend is in there ready to tear the house down. He's been worried about you."

As if he could sense they were talking about him, Adam stepped out of the house and stalked toward them. His lips were drawn into a thin line and his blond brows were matching parallel lines as his eyes blazed with an ever-changing mix of emotions. A series of grunts and growls erupted from his throat as he hauled her against him and laid a kiss on her that tasted of desperation, need, and fear. His fingers dug into her biceps and his teeth were sharp on her lips.

It was then that she realized how childish she had been, storming out of the house without a single word of explanation. If the situation were reversed, she sure as hell wouldn't be kissing him, at least not with her lips. The sole of her boot, however, would have that privilege.

She wrapped her arms around his waist and held him tight, moving her hands up and down his back in an attempt to ease the beast. The soothing motion appeared to do the trick as he sighed against her lips and pulled back enough to touch his forehead to her.

"I'm sorry I wasn't there for you." Anguish roughed up his tone to a low warble.

"I'm sorry I ran away."

"Where did you go?"

"Away. I needed to cool off. Talked with Megan for a while."

His breath hitched and he grew real still. "About leaving Mission? Yeah, I had heard that much this morning. You want to leave Mission. Leave me."

How was she to answer? Yes, a good portion of their conversation had been making plans for her future. A trip to New York. Compiling a list of towns to move to for a while before moving on to someplace else exciting. The possibility and hope for more made her heart happy and eased the ache of Stacy's bullying.

But that happiness had been but a cake-pop compared to the ten-tier wedding cake amount of joy she had felt telling Megan about Adam. How he made her smile, how beautiful he made her feel. And with each word, the thought of leaving hurt just as much as the thought of staying. Yes, she wanted to be with Adam. But how long until the oppression of living in Mission dragged her down to the point where she began to despise him?

"Adam, the best thing about Mission is you. Never doubt that."

A wary grin curled the corner of his lips. "I don't know if that's a good or bad thing, considering how much I know you hate this town."

"It's a good thing." She went on her tiptoes to press a kiss to the corner of his mouth.

The rumble of an engine caught her attention as an SUV pulled up behind Adam's truck. Gabriella and Faith jumped out of the car.

"Well," he said, sighing. "Looks like the cavalry showed up."

"What's going on?" she asked.

"Nic, honey," Faith said as she climbed the front steps.

"How you holding up?"

"Do you want me to rearrange Stacy's face?" Gabriella asked. "I can make that happen."

Nic turned a questioning gaze to Adam, whose cheeks flushed pink. He rubbed at his jaw and shrugged. "Sorry. Jack and I had to tell Trey where we were going. Greta must have overheard."

The horn of the SUV blared and they all turned to see Greta in the front seat with a big smile on her face, waving at them with both hands.

Holy hell. As usual, good news traveled fast in Mission.

A sigh of both frustration and amusement caught Nic by surprise. "I'm fine. Really. Maiming anyone on my behalf is not required."

"Are you sure?" Gabriela started cracking the knuckles on one of her hands. "No one messes with my friend."

"I'm sure. But thank you for the thought."

"I hope your schedule is clear for the day," Faith said with a sweep of her hand. "You are coming with us for a girls' day at the spa."

"Oh. Wow. Um, thank you for asking, but I can't go. It's been a long morning, and I need to help out my aunt Jacqui."

"But it's Sunday," she said. "Aren't you closed on Sundays?"

"We are, but there are lots of other things that need to be done, too."

Like watching her mother. Aunt Jacqui had been great about giving her time to spend with Adam, but the woman couldn't take all of the burden. That wasn't fair.

"I'll stay," Adam offered.

"Me, too," Jack said.

"What? Oh, no. I can't ask you guys to do that."

"We want to," Adam said. "It'll give me a chance to sweet-talk your family some more." He flashed her a wink.

"And it looks like you have a few things that could be done around the house," Jack added. "Your air-conditioner sounds like it's working too hard. You definitely don't want that to go out with this summer heat. Besides, your mom is a hoot."

Nic looked to Adam and raised her eyebrows in question.

He gave her a small smile and nodded. "She's having a good day."

"Please come with us, Nic," Faith pleaded with her hands pressed beneath her chin and fluttered her lashes. "Please."

"But what about your work?" she asked the fellas.

"Got it covered," Gabriella said with cell phone already in hand. "I know the boss pretty well."

"Make a pregnant woman happy and come with us," Greta shouted from the car.

What a way to box a person in.

With five hopeful faces staring at her, she didn't want to be the petulant child and say no. Especially when she really wanted to leave the pity party in the past and have some fun.

"Sure, why not. But I can't be out too long. Just let me drop my bag off. I'll be right back."

She ran up to her room and lingered only long enough to drop off her overnight bag and redress herself in a more comfortable manner. Not even she was brave enough to spend the day out going commando.

When she was dressed and felt more like herself, she ran back down the stairs to see her mother laughing with Jack.

Marie's eyes lit up as she spotted Nic. "Hi, sweetie, I made a new friend."

"You did? That's great."

"Yep. Jack here is going to fix Grandpa's rocking chair so it doesn't squeak anymore, and fix the lock in my bedroom window so I can open it again."

Nic caught Jack's gaze. "That's great about the *rocking chair,*" she emphasized and shook her head when she added, "And the lock on the window."

Jack's eyebrows popped up for a second before he nodded with understanding. "Is there anything else you like for me to do while I'm here, Miss Marie?"

"Yes," she added with her finger raised in the air. "There's a fairy trapped in the wall of my room. Can you please get her out and see her safely home?"

Jack didn't even bat an eye. "I sure will, ma'am."

"Mom, I'm going to be out for a little while longer, will you be good for the boys?"

"Oh, yes." She made a crossing motion over her heart. "It's been so long since I've entertained such handsome gentlemen. We're going to have great fun."

Nic turned to Adam and grabbed him by the front of his shirt, hauling him close until they were nose to nose. "You call me if you need anything. *Anything.* And don't make it so Aunt Jacqui is taking care of the three of you."

"Of course." He rubbed his palms up and down her arms and the top of her shoulders. "Have fun. It means a lot to me that you're going out with the girls."

"I like them, Adam. And I know they're important to you."

"You're important to me, too." He kissed her forehead then nuzzled his nose against hers. "You're getting to be the most important thing in my life," he whispered, and a lump filled her throat and her eyes stung.

"You're pretty special to me, too," she whispered back.

A light of desire flashed in his eyes that took her breath away. Throwing decorum out the wind, he took her mouth with a deep passionate kiss that was doing a damn fine job of convincing her to drag him upstairs to her room and lock the door for at least a week.

"Condoms," Marie yelled, grabbing the notepad out of Jack's hand and throwing it at them.

Jack burst out laughing and fell onto his side, with his arms wrapped around his waist.

Nic gave Adam one last hug then went to kiss her mother's cheek. "Love ya, Mom."

"'Bye, sweetie."

"Aunt Jacqui, do you need me to pick up anything while I'm out?"

"We're fine," she said from the doorway of the kitchen. "Have fun."

With one hand on the front door, she paused for one last look at her family. Marie was flirting with Jack while Adam was sweet-talking her aunt into making a batch or three of brownies. It wouldn't surprise Nic one bit to come home to find the huge dining room table covered with every dessert from the bakery's display case, a bite taken out of each one.

"Thanks for waiting," she said to the girls as she took her seat in the back of the SUV. "I'm not sure who needs the supervision, my mother or the guys."

"Maybe they'll keep each other in line," Greta replied. "I'm so glad you're coming with us. I only wish Melody could have joined us."

"Where is she?" Faith asked.

"She's at a retreat for elementary school teachers in Chelan for the week," Gabriella answered. "It's supposed to be hotter there than here by ten degrees. She wasn't looking forward to it."

"Ugh." Greta twisted her lips in disgust. "That sounds miserable. And speaking of miserable, I really try not to speak ill of people, but man, that Stacy is a bitch. What happened? Did she really attack you?"

"I don't know what she was doing." Nic shook her head. "But it wasn't pleasant. Doesn't matter. It's over now."

Greta sighed and shook her head. "What has gotten into this town lately? When I moved here, everyone was relaxed and groovy. Now they're all uptight and twitchy."

"They're all jealous," Gabriella replied. "Because we're all so freaking happy. They want what we have, but aren't willing to do what it takes to get it."

The three women shared a smile of camaraderie and affection that came with experiencing love for another with one's entire heart and soul.

Nic felt her lips stretch to match their wide grins, beginning to understand that type of power.

The forty-five-minute drive into Yakima passed quickly amidst the miles of laughter and companionship.

"Oh, Miner Burgers," Greta sighed with longing and rubbed her belly as they passed the drive-in. "Let's have a spa day there. Baby wants fries and fry sauce."

"Later, mama. I promise," Gabriella replied. "But let's not tell the boys. They'll be sad we didn't bring them back anything, but there is no way a milkshake is going to make the trip home."

The mall was packed with after-church shoppers, and the parking lot was crazy crowded. Greta pulled a parking placard with a triumphant hoot and placed it over the rearview mirror. "Being pregnant does have its perks."

Faith led the way to the day spa that was owned by one of her former beauty school classmates, who welcomed them all with hugs and glasses of champagne—orange juice for Greta— when they walked through the door.

The last time Nic had had a mani and pedi was the week

before she left for Mission, and she and Megan had spent the day going to all the types of places the sleepy town didn't have—museums, the theater, seafood restaurants. It had been one of the happiest and saddest days of her life.

Now there she was, in the middle of the arid central Washington landscape with her toes soaking in a bubbling tub laughing at one of Faith's stories. While she missed Megan and the rest of her friends something fierce, being in the company of these women was just as joyful.

"Ooo," Greta gasped and clutched at her belly. The girl massaging her feet froze and they all stared at Greta as if she were about to explode until she let out a slow breath. "It's okay. We're okay. I've heard that massages can put a woman into labor."

"Oh my gosh," the esthetician exclaimed. "Let's move on to something else."

"No," Greta shouted. "I'm ready to have this baby. Massage away."

"Are you sure?" Gabriella asked. "The other day you were saying you want to be pregnant forever."

Greta waved a dismissive hand. "That was just the hormones talking. I'm ready. I think I'm ready. I'm mostly ready. Ask me again in ten minutes."

A hush fell across the room that Nic didn't fully understand, but the concern in Gabriella's and Faith's eyes was enough to make her throat tighten in sympathy.

Gabriella reached across the console and grabbed Greta's hand. "The baby is going to be fine. You're going to be fine. And Trey is going to be fine. Even if I have to kick his ass, he will be fine."

"I know," Greta said and offered a strained smile. "I have to stop thinking that this baby will suffer the same fate as Luke. But

I can't help a stray thought coming in, well, almost every hour."

Ah, now Nic understood the somber mood that had suddenly fallen. She had heard the story about little Luke Armstrong, who had passed away at far, far, far too young an age.

To unexpectedly lose a child was a nightmare she couldn't fathom. Then to have to live with the fear it could happen again had to be a terrible burden that tested one's faith. The fact that Greta fluctuated between joy and despair yet found a reason to smile was a testament to her strength.

"Colby wants a baby," Faith admitted so quietly they almost didn't hear her over the sound of the bubbling foot spas. "And I do, too. He doesn't care if it's his or Ben's, although I think we both want it to be Ben's."

"Ben doesn't want children?" Greta asked.

"He thinks he's too old to start becoming a father. Maybe he's right. But the thought of having a little bit of him on this earth when we're all gone makes my heart happy." She reached up and dabbed at the tears collecting on her eyelashes with the corner of a napkin.

Nic couldn't stop the trickle of laughter that bubbled past her lips. When the other women looked at her in question, she shook her head. "I'm sorry. It's not every day you hear about a man telling his girlfriend to have another man's baby."

Faith chuckled. "I know. I am incredibly lucky. I wouldn't trade my two men in for normalcy ever. Ever ever."

Gabriella raised her glass. "A toast. May we always have the courage to go after what makes us happy, and to hell with those who try to stop us. And to the friends who stand by us on our journey. No matter what."

"Hear, hear," Faith cheered.

"You guys are the best," Greta sobbed and dabbed at her face with the sleeves of her robe and raised her glass of juice.

Nic took a sip of champagne and felt the carbonation burn a line of fire from her throat down to her belly. To be included in this circle of amazing women was both humbling and empowering. These women fought like hell to be with the men they loved. Their spirit was undeniable.

But to sit with them while she had not a few hours earlier contemplated how to let the man she loved go made her feel like an impostor among them.

"You're awfully quiet there, Nic," said Greta. "Are we embarrassing you with all of our gushing?"

"Not at all." She swallowed past the lump in her throat. "What you all have, the three of you together, I mean, is really special. True friends are hard to find. You're lucky."

"We count you as a friend too."

"I appreciate that." She bit her lip. "Thank you."

It was on the tip of her tongue to spill her concerns about Adam, so much so that she had to suck in her lips to trap the words behind her teeth.

There was only so much she was willing to blurt out to others. Even when they made a gesture indicating they were willing to listen. For now, her troubles were her own. Tomorrow was soon enough to make a decision.

Chapter Thirteen

A NY FEARS NIC had about the state of her home were settled the moment she walked in the front door.

Adam, Jack, and her mother were all seated at the dining room table. Sugar cookies in various shapes and sizes were laid out on plates before them. A rainbow of sprinkles was spread across the table in front of the boys, who each had smudges of icing on their cheeks and down the front of their shirts.

The corner of the table where her mother sat was immaculate. Three separate piping bags, each filled with red, white, and blue icing, sat in glasses in front of her. There was a line of demarcation separating her work area from the boys, as if she had dared the sugar sprinkle mess to cross into her space.

To Marie's side, she had a tray of cookies laid out in neat rows, each one decorated with swirls and lines and topped with just the right amount of sugar to make them worthy to be photographed in a culinary magazine. Nic couldn't remember the last time she had seen her mother work so diligently, with her head down and her gaze laser focused on the task.

"Nic," her aunt greeted as she swept in from the kitchen with another tray of freshly baked cookies in her hands. "How was the spa?"

Nic had to blink a few times before tearing her gaze away from her mother, who had yet to look up from her work. "It was good. Fun."

"Are you all fresh and polished?"

"Most definitely. Looks like you all have quite a project going on here."

"The boys helped out so much around the house, I thought they deserved a treat."

"Looks like this treat is creating more work for you."

"Oh." Her aunt waved a dismissive hand. "It's been fun watching them."

"Hey, sweetness," Adam said and held up his latest masterpiece. "Check it out."

The lettering was far from perfect, but the words "Eat me" were clearly legible.

"Classy," she said with a chuckle.

"I also made some with an 'A' and an 'N' on them." He pointed to a plate of hearts with their initials sprawled across the top.

"Sampled a few of them, too, I see." She reached for a napkin to remove a glob of icing from the corner of his mouth. "How many have you eaten?"

He shared a glance with Jack. "We lost track after about a dozen. Each. They're really good."

Jack began to giggle with an almost maniacal tone. "I've never had so much sugar in my life. I think my heart is going to explode."

Her mother looked up from her work and gasped as she spotted her daughter. "Nic, when did you get home?"

"A few minutes ago. Those are excellent, Mom."

Her mother blinked a few times then looked down at the table where Nic was pointing. "Oh my goodness. These are beautiful. Who did these?"

Nic walked over to her mother and laid a hand on her shoulder. "You did, Mom."

"I did?" She blinked again and her eyes searched the room. A nervous smile twisted her lips.

"How was your day?" Nic asked, eager to replace the lost look in her mother's eyes.

"Good. I made some new friends. This is Jack and Adam." She leaned closer to whisper in a not so quiet voice. "Adam has a girlfriend he loves something fierce. But Jack is single. You should ask him out."

"I'm already dating someone, Mom."

"You are?" her mother drew back in surprise. "Who?"

"Adam."

Understanding crept slowly across Marie's face and her eyes lit up with joy. "That's wonderful," she exclaimed.

"Can I start putting some of these things away and get you some dinner? You should probably have something to eat in the vegetable food group."

Jacqui chimed in. "I have a lasagna in the oven. It should be ready in about ten minutes."

"Would you like me to start a salad?"

"Sure."

"What are we having for dessert?" Adam asked, clapping his hands together with glee.

"Haven't you had enough sugar?"

"I will always have room for some of your sweets, sweet."

"Then I think the perfect dessert for tonight would be a nice bowl of fruit."

Adam and Jack both gasped and their mouths fell open as if she just shut the door in their faces.

"That doesn't sound exciting at all," Adam said.

"Fruit can be fun. Especially if you add liquor to it. My favorite dessert is cherries jubilee. It's warm and sweet and goes awesomely on almost everything."

"I vote for that," Adam said and Jack nodded enthusiastically.

"I feel like I'm your mother trying to encourage you to eat healthy. But you are adults." She snorted. "*I* will be having fruit. It's up to Aunt Jacqui if she wants to feed you anything else."

The boys turned toward her aunt and batted their long lashes at her. Of course the woman caved in an instant. "I have brownies."

The boys whooped and hollered, then toasted each other with another sugar cookie each that they then scarfed down.

With Jack and Adam at their table, dinner reminded Nic of her childhood when friends and family were always on hand to share a meal. She hadn't seen her aunt Jacqui look so relaxed and happy in a long time. The line of strain that usually bracketed her mouth softened as she giggled like a teenager over the two cowboys.

Even her mother was at her most serene. Marie watched the conversation with rapt attention. A little smile played on her lips, and every now and again, her eyes gleamed with happy tears as she clapped whenever the men hit an exciting part of their stories.

But as was wont to happen, all good things had to come to an end, and soon there was nothing but empty dishes and crumbs left on the table.

"I don't see where you boys put all these calories," Aunt Jacqui said with a shake of her head.

"We find ways to burn them off," Adam replied with a chuckle and snatched Nic around the waist to pull her in for a hug.

"Come home with me tonight?" he asked in her ear. "I've missed you today."

The idea was not without its merit, but she shook her head, determined to be responsible. "I need to stay with my family tonight. It's been a big day for Mom."

"Tomorrow?" he asked. "Or the next night, or the next night? I need you."

"You make it so hard to say no." She gave him one last peck on the cheek then pushed him away. "I'll think about it."

"Of course." He turned those big cow eyes on her. "I can stay here? I can run Jack back to the ranch and come back here to you."

"Sneak a boy into my room? I haven't done that in—" She broke off when he shot her a stunned look. "If you want to make the drive, I'd open the door for you."

"Hot damn." He smacked a quick kiss to her lips. "I will fly like the wind."

"Safely. Please drive safely."

"Anything for you, sweetness." He turned toward his buddy. "Jack, let's hit the road. I have plans for later."

"Thanks for the wonderful day, ladies." Jack took a hold of Marie's hand and pressed a kiss to her knuckles. He whistled in appreciation when Jacqui handed him a plate of cookies all wrapped with a blue ribbon. "For me? Aww, no way."

"Of course for you. Which you will share with Adam," Jacqui added with a laugh. "You boys worked hard to make them."

"You ladies are the best." He leaned over and kissed her cheek. "Adam, we need to come back more often."

"I'm planning on it. And we're not telling anyone about those cookies. Keep them in the car or else Rafe will steal them all."

"Good thinking."

After more hugs and kisses good-bye, the three Fournier/Devereux women stood on the front porch and watched as the cowboys drove off into the sunset.

Marie sighed with contentment. "That was a good day."

Nic looked over her mother's head and shared a relieved glance with her aunt. "Yeah. It was a good day."

Walking back into the house, the absence of the men and their boisterous laughter reminded Nic of a balloon after all of the helium had leaked out. The house was silent. Flat. Almost melancholy.

"I don't know about you," Jacqui said as she flopped into an armchair. "I am beat. Those boys have a lot of energy. You have a good man there, Nic."

"Thanks. He is pretty cool. Come on, Mom. Let's get you ready for bed. You've had a big day."

She followed her mother up the stairs and guided her into the bathroom. Together they cleaned their teeth, and Nic brushed out her mother's hair. If left on her own, Marie would take hours getting ready for bed, easily becoming distracted by the way the faucets worked, or how the toilet flushed, or how the shower spouted.

Once all of their personal needs were taken care of, they moved on to Marie's room, where Nic pulled out her mother's pajamas and set them on the bed.

"Do you need help dressing, Mom?" Marie shook her head. "Then I'm going to change. I'll be right back."

"Right back" was less than two minutes, but it might as well have been an hour, considering the amount of damage her mother had done to her room. Dresser drawers had been opened, clothes strewn haphazardly around the room. The pillows and bedding had been tossed on the floor, and her mother was bent over, with her head in the closet, throwing clothes out over her shoulder.

"Mom. What are you doing?"

"I can't find them," she replied with a watery hitch in her voice. "They were here a minute ago and now they're gone."

"What's gone? What are you looking for?"

"My dolls."

"What dolls?"

"My cowboy dolls." Her mother stepped out of the closet with tears running down her face. "My two cowboys. They were here a minute ago. I wanted to sleep with them. They make me feel safe."

"Mom. You don't have any dolls."

"I do," she shouted. "Two of them. I named them Jack and Adam. I had them and now they're gone."

Oh, no. Apparently it was too much to ask the powers that be to end the night on a high note.

"They were right here. I played with them all day." Marie suddenly stopped pacing and looked at Nic with suspicion. "Did you take them? You did, didn't you? Give them back!"

"I didn't take anything. Those weren't dolls, Mother, those were my friends. I can call them on the phone and they can talk to you. Tell you that they're okay."

"Give them back," her mother screamed and leapt the small distance with her fingers curled into claws. "Give them back!"

This wasn't the first time her mother had struck out at her, or the most violent. But after the day Marie had had, having been lucid most of the time, the attack knocked Nic for a loop, scrambling her train of thought about how to best defuse the situation.

Nic threw her hands up, more in self-defense than aggression. "Mom, stop. Please stop."

Allowing hysteria to control her actions was not going to help either of them, but the frustration clawing within her cut just as sharply as her mother's fingernails. The pounding of footsteps came from down the hall, and soon Jacqui was there to assist, wrapping her arms around Marie's middle. Nic dropped her hands for the half second needed for Marie to take a swing. The crack of fist hitting cheek was like a gunshot in the room, and everyone froze as if someone had hit pause on a remote control.

Then as one, they moved. Slowly. Frame by frame. A blink of an eye. An intake of breath, until Nic met her mother's stunned gaze.

"Nicolette?" The clouds in Marie's eyes cleared and she wilted in her sister's arms. "What happened?" She glanced around at the total destruction of her room. "What is happening?"

"You forgot, Mother." Nic lifted her hand to touch the sore spot on her face, but she paused, not wanting to draw attention to the injury. "You forgot. We were getting ready for bed."

"Oh, Nic," her mother sobbed. "What have I done?"

"It's nothing. Just a misunderstanding." Nic reached out and grabbed her mother's limp hands and pulled them against her chest. "Why don't you put on your pajamas, and Aunt Jacqui and I will get your room back together. Okay?" She leaned and pressed a kiss to her mother's wet cheek.

It was as if her mother shrunk, becoming a child once again. She whimpered and nodded her head and accepted the set of pajamas Jacqui had picked up from the floor. The women were silent, except for a sniffle now and again from Marie as they quickly worked to put the room back together into some semblance of order. A more thorough cleanup would have to wait until the morning.

There was no denying it anymore. Marie's dementia was getting worse and worse. Those sparks of recognition, the glimmers of the mother Nic remembered, were becoming fewer and far between. Although no words were spoken, the meaningful glance Jacqui sent her way conveyed they shared the same thought. The two of them were not going to be enough to keep Marie safe.

Her mother climbed into bed and curled into a ball the moment her head hit the pillow. Nic brought the blanket up under her chin and tucked it around her mother's shoulders.

"Good night, Mom. I love you."

As she straightened to turn away, Marie's hand shot out and latched onto her wrist. "I love you, Nicolette. I love you more than anything."

"I know, Mom." She laid her hand on her mother's head and gave her a bittersweet smile. "Sweet dreams."

"Nic," Jacqui started when Nic joined her in the hallway.

"Tomorrow, Aunt Jacqui. We'll talk tomorrow."

Jacqui's eyes teared up as she nodded. "Good night, sweetie."

For a woman who preferred to keep an even keel, Nic's day had been a clusterfuck of riotous emotions. Who decided to set her in the middle of a parachute and have a class of kindergarteners toss her until she lost her cookies? Her brain was fried. Shot. Kaput.

Thank God for routine. Muscle memory got her through the task of brushing her teeth and dressing for bed. Only the blaring notes of "Save a Horse, Ride a Cowboy" coming from her phone woke her from her waking sleep.

"Hey, Adam," she said when she answered the phone.

"Where are you? I've been texting you."

"Oh. Sorry. I didn't hear or see them. Are you on your way?"

"I'm here. I'm outside your door. I didn't want to knock and wake anyone."

Crap. Had it really been that long since he left? "I'll be down in a second."

On her way to the stairs, she took a detour to her mother's room and opened the door just enough to peer inside. Marie had kicked off all of her blankets and lay sprawled across the mattress in a shape of a star. The soft hiccup of her snores drifted across the room, making Nic smile.

After closing the door, she crept down the stairs to let Adam in. His big grin dropped and his brows furrowed the moment the light from the porch hit her face.

"What happened?" he asked and hovered the tips of his fingers over her swollen cheek.

"Mom had an episode."

"Ah, sweetness. I'm sorry. She was doing so well today."

Nic shrugged. "It's just one of those things. Do you—Would you be willing to just hold me tonight? I'm really not in the mood for sex."

Adam sighed and leaned against the doorframe. "Darling, I don't care what we're doing as long as I'm with you. Whatever you need, I'm there."

"Thanks." She kissed his cheek and took him by the hand.

Neither of them spoke as they returned to her room. She climbed into bed and watched with sleepy appreciation as he stripped down to his boxers.

The moment he settled into bed, he pulled her into the cradle of his arms. With her head cushioned on his solid chest, his heartbeat was a strong and steady metronome lulling her to sleep.

That was Adam. Strong, steady, hardworking, breathing life into everything he touched.

Despite their exhaustion, they didn't fall asleep for the longest time. They lay there for who knew how long, trading caresses and soft sighs. Every once in a while, he would press a kiss to her forehead or the tip of her nose as he ran his hands up and down her back and across her arms, swirling circular patterns over her skin. The love he felt for her was there in his touch. But as she had taught him to do, he didn't say the words she saw shining in his eyes.

Funny thing was, she didn't need them. It was all there in his actions. The way he cared for his family. The way he cared for *her* family. The way he treated her as if she were precious. Adam was a man who loved, and loved fiercely. A rare find in a world where talk was cheap and one's actions were inconsequential.

Sleep was a worthy opponent and finally chiseled away at the barriers of her stress to sweep her away to dark slumber. Slowly, oh so slowly, she sank into its murky depths. Just as she succumbed to the delicious lull, she was jerked awake as if she were a fish snared on a fisherman's hook and whipped up to the surface.

"Wha—?" she gasped.

"Nic." Adam's voice was sharp with alarm, sending goose bumps up her arms. "Wake up."

She sat up and instantly choked as she sucked in a lungful of something harsh and hot.

The room was pitch dark, and the air around her felt heavy, unnatural.

"Come on, Nic. Let's go."

Adam's shoulders were a darker blur in the night. "What's going on? Why are you on the floor?"

"Sweetness, I think your house is on fire."

Chapter Fourteen

NIC BOLTED TO her knees and swung her legs over the side of the bed. The scant moonlight coming through the window did jack-shit to penetrate the darkness. All was silent. Deathly silent with only the stench of burning metal and fabric confirming the fire was close by.

She was just about to stand when Adam hauled her to the floor.

"Stay low where the air's not so bad," he said.

"Why aren't the smoke alarms going off?"

"The power's out," he replied. "I tried the lights and they didn't work. When was the last time you changed the batteries on the manual alarms?"

"Crap. I don't remember."

He tapped her on the shoulder and guided her to follow him as they crawled across the floor. In the hallway, Adam turned left toward the stairs.

She grabbed him by the ankle. "Wait. Where's my mother?"

"I don't know. Nic. Nic? Where are you?"

But she was already gone, scrambling on hands and knees as fast as she was able to her mother's room and reached out with a blind hand for the door. It was already open.

"Mom," she called out. "Mom, are you there?"

She dared to climb to her feet, but stayed in a low crouch as she made her way to the bed and felt along the mattress. Nothing but bed sheets and blankets. Hopefully, her mother had already gone downstairs and was waiting for her outside.

"Nic. Come on," Adam shouted from the top of the stairs.

"I'm coming."

With each step to the stairs, the silence gave way to the crackle and pop of flames eating the house as if it were a bowl of potato chips. As they reached the bottom of the stairs, an orange glow flickered, making the remaining darkness appear more black and ominous, reminding her of photos of deep space.

"Oh my God," Adam exclaimed and Nic felt her heart slam into her chest at the sight of the red-yellow flames licking at the doorway to the kitchen.

Great billowy clouds of smoke rolled and undulated across the ceiling, growing thicker by the second. The rolling mass hypnotized her with its deadly dance, robbing her of the ability to move as the life-sucking fumes stole into her lungs. Only Adam's hand on her arm pulled her away from the horror.

"Let's get out of here."

He tugged her toward the front door that stood wide open. In comparison to the heat inside the home, the warm August night air was a welcome relief.

In a tangle of arms and legs, they tumbled down the stairs, until she landed on her knees in the grass, sucking in big, deep gulps of dry air.

"Nic," a female voice shouted over the raucous noise of her coughing fit.

"Aunt Jacqui?" she squeaked.

Jacqui's hands were cool on her back. "Have you seen your mother? I can't find Marie."

Spots floated in Nic's vision as she tried to focus. Besides the few street lamps, the only source of light was the orange flames shooting up from the backside of the house.

Oh no. The bakery.

Her legs felt as strong as a toothpick holding up a cinnamon roll as she tried to stand. "The bakery. Mom. She wasn't in her room."

"Then where is she?"

"I'll find her," Adam said and was gone in a flash.

"Adam," she shouted as he ran back to the house.

He paused by the front door and shouted for her mother before disappearing inside.

"No," she screamed and made a move to run after him, only to be held back by Jacqui's arms around her.

"Nic, you can't. It's not safe."

Flashing lights of red and blue painted the night like paintballs hitting a canvas as the police appeared, followed closely by two fire engines.

Nic shook free from Jacqui's hold and ran to the porch. A wall of heat stopped her in her tracks as she screamed for her mother and Adam.

"Ma'am, you have to get back."

Hands much rougher and stronger than her aunt's grabbed her by the arms and hauled her off the porch. She didn't know who the hands belonged to. Didn't see his face. Didn't even bother to look. Her attention was focused solely on the open front door and the plumes of smoke billowing out of the opening.

"Adam," she screamed. "Adam."

His name echoed over and over in her head, drowning out the shouts of men and women hurrying to put the fire out.

Two firefighters approached the front door, only to draw

back as a figure emerged from the dark.

Adam stumbled down the stairs and collapsed onto the grass with Marie clutched in his arms. He rolled to his side, coughing and gasping, his face streaked with soot and tears.

"Oh my God." Nic dropped to her knees beside them. She waved her arms about in a frantic arc, unsure what or where to touch to offer assistance.

Soot covered her mother from head to toe. Her nightgown had melted to her skin and most of her hair was burned clean off.

"Oh God, Mother. Mom."

Marie's lashes fluttered and her lips moved, but the garbled sound was barely audible.

Adam's hand landed on her thigh, making her jump in surprise.

"She," he paused to cough. "Was in the bakery kitchen. Cherries jubilee. Kept repeating. Cherries jubilee."

What the fuck did that mean?

Paramedics surrounded them, but Adam waved them away. "Get Marie first. Get her first."

Her mother reached out and latched onto Nic's wrist with surprising strength. Her eyes cracked open, exposing bloodshot irises. "I'm sorry." Her cracked lips formed the words.

Nic leaned closer, unable to make out what her mother was saying with all of the shouting and commotion around her.

"Sorry," her mother said again.

"It's okay, Mom." She tried not to squeeze her mother's fingers too tight. "Help is here."

Marie tugged her hand away from Nic's grasp and reached for Adam, bringing his hand around to clasp her daughter's. "Care. Of her. Love her."

"I promise."

The corners of her lips trembled then were obscured altogether as the paramedics slipped an oxygen mask over her face and lifted her onto a gurney. Her eyelids fluttered shut and she appeared to wilt as her grip weakened and fell away.

No, no, no, no!

Nic rose and tried to chase after the paramedics as they whisked her mother into the back of the ambulance. Medical jargon she didn't understand was shouted in terse voices. But what she could comprehend was the grim looks on their faces. Determination set their lips into solid lines, but the hopelessness in their eyes was apparent.

Nic had barely settled onto the bench seat before the ambulance took off, knocking her off balance and into the paramedic beside her. The woman didn't even register the contact, keeping her focus entirely on Marie as she secured sensors on her raw chest.

No one, not even Nic, was surprised when they turned on the heart monitor and nothing but a solid line appeared on the screen.

Chapter Fifteen

THE SUNSET PUT on a spectacular show of orange and purple that streaked across the sky in wavy lines as if the clouds were saying good night to the mountains. A gentle breeze kicked up, caressing Nic with warm fingers, but a chill had set into her bones that not even the eighty-degree evening air could thaw.

Greta and Trey had been generous enough to offer Nic and her aunt a place to stay after the fire destroyed their home. Every night for the last few weeks, Nic had ended the day sitting on the wide porch swing, rocking and staring into the vast prairie. If anyone asked her what she was thinking, "Nothing" was her reply.

Sometimes it was nothing. Other times, past conversations played in her mind. And then there were the what-ifs. Had there been a way to save her mother? What if they had put her in a hospital when she first showed signs of illness? What more could she have done to keep them all safe?

But most of the time it was nothing. Just her. Sitting. Rocking. Breathing. Listening to the sounds of the ranch, and nature, and the world as it continued to turn as it had for millions of years, and would continue to turn forever more.

Sometimes Adam joined her, other times it was her aunt.

Never did they try to force her to make conversation, content to allow her time to sit and just be.

In her heart and in her head, Nic knew she'd have to rejoin the living at some point, and some point soon, but the energy to take action eluded her. For so long she had wished for the freedom to do whatever she wanted. Now that the time had arrived, she'd do anything to give it back and have her mother by her side.

Careful what you wish for, the saying went. If anyone needed a poster child for that warning, she'd be on the swing, every night for the foreseeable future.

"There's my girl," Adam said as he climbed the front steps with Jacqui following. The giant accordion file in her aunt's arms set a wave of guilt that tightened around Nic's chest.

"How did it go with the lawyers?" she asked, knowing she should have been with her aunt to settle her mother's affairs.

"Good." Jacqui joined her on the swing. "Insurance is going to cover everything. And your mother had a life insurance policy. It's enough for me to rebuild and open the shop again. She also had some money set aside for you."

"That's great." She hoped her smile matched her genuine pleasure at the news.

Jacqui balanced the file on her lap and reached out to grasp both of Nic's hands. "Nic, I want you..." she trailed off and her gaze switched between Nic and Adam. "I have more news to share. But we can discuss it later. I'm going to go in, freshen up a bit, and see if Gabriella needs any help with dinner."

With a quick kiss to Nic's cheek, she left the two of them alone. Adam watched her with his hat in his hands. A thousand questions burned in his eyes, yet he allowed her to sit in silence.

"Thank you for going with Jacqui," she said. "I couldn't—I wasn't ready." She placed her hand on the center of her chest and pushed, trying to quell the burning sensation in her sternum that ignited every time she thought about moving on.

"I know," he said and took the seat Jacqui vacated. He rested his arm along the back of the swing. "There isn't a start and end date for grieving, Nic. You take all the time you need."

"That's just it. Time is one of those things we have either in abundance or not enough. I know life is marching on, and I want to march on, too. But I can't seem to find the will to be productive."

"No one's asking you to, sweetness."

"I know. I know."

Everyone at the ranch had been wonderful, allowing her to be among them without being "present." No one was in her face, asking her if she wanted to talk about her feelings or telling her to buck up and be brave. They didn't treat her as if she were broken, but they didn't handle her with kid gloves, either. They simply went about their day and treated her with courtesy.

And Adam, oh Adam had been more than supportive. Whatever she needed, he provided. Whether she needed a tissue, a glass of water, or a hug, he was there.

Most nights, he slept by her side, wrapping her in his strong arms. But on occasion, she needed more than a gentle touch. She needed to forget. Needed hot and frenzied. Sex for sex's sake in order to feel something other than numbness, and Adam provided. And when she was done screaming her orgasm into the universe, he'd catch her on the fall back to earth, holding her as she cried until dawn.

"Thank you," she said, and rested her hand on his thigh. "Thank you for letting me float day to day. The thing is, I don't want to float. I want to move on. I just don't know where to start."

He nodded and a veil of sadness washed across his face as

his lips pinched together. The sudden seriousness to his demeanor put her on edge, and she held her breath as she waited for him to say what was on his mind.

"I, uh." He paused to clear his throat. "I have something for you that may help you decide."

As he reached into his front pocket, her already full lungs tried to suck in more air. Her vision swam as she verged on the edge of hyperventilating. Holy crap. Was he going to propose?

But it wasn't a ring he withdrew from his pocket, but a folded-up piece of paper.

All of the air she held whooshed out in a blast of...disappointment? Was she really disappointed Adam wasn't going to ask her to marry him?

Yes. Yes, she was.

"What's this?" she asked, taking the paper. Confusion made it impossible for her to read whatever was written.

"It's a plane ticket. For Paris."

He might as well have punched her in the chest, for she was equally as stunned. "Paris? You're sending me away?"

"I'm setting you free, babe." He gestured to the wide expanse of ranch land around them. "Mission has brought you nothing but heartache and bad memories. Your light is too bright to keep you here. You need to go and be happy."

Never before had a single piece of paper felt so heavy. She balanced the sheet in her hand and watched it as if it would explode at any minute.

Adam had literally given her a ticket to freedom. He was right. Nothing tied her Mission anymore. Nothing but him.

But didn't he realize? He was everything.

"It's all arranged," he was saying. Talking more to the toe of his boot than to her. "You just need to get your passport reissued, which is why your trip isn't for a while now. But first, you're going to have to stop in New York for a few days. Megan will be ready for you."

"Megan?"

"Yeah, we put it all together when she was here for the funeral."

A familiar sting of tears burned her eyes, knowing her best friend and Adam worked together to provide her with her greatest wish. "I don't know what to say."

"I don't know either, darling. Part of me wants to tell you to go on and forget all about me, but that's not true." He shook his head. "Write to me. Share your adventures with me. Don't forget the cowboy in the small town who only wanted for you to be happy."

"But, Adam." His words made her body curl into itself as if she had just been stabbed in the chest. "I don't want to forget about you. And I don't want to leave you. But you're right about this town. It's like it's trying to suck my soul."

"Then go." He grabbed both of her hands in his, crushing the paper in his grip. "Go and be amazing."

Careful what you wish for. Careful what you wish for. Careful what you wish for.

No, no, no. This was wrong. It was all wrong.

While going off on one's own might sound great in theory, adventures were only as good as the people you shared them with. To some, climbing Mount Everest was an adventure. To others, negotiating the Tube system in London was equally as grand. Then there were those who considered trying the new restaurant down the street as much of an adventure as exploring Antarctica.

And the funny thing was, they were all right. If you were with the right person, anything could be an adventure.

"What about you?" she asked quietly.

"What about me?" He shrugged. "I'll be here. Nursing a broken heart. Wishing I were enough."

She slapped him on the arm. "You fucker. You *are* enough. Have you any idea how completely wonderful you are? I love you, Adam. All right? I love you." Hysterical laughter bubbled past her lips. "I don't want to leave *you*. I want to be with you."

"I want to be with you, too. I love you, Nic. I've loved you from the moment you came down that ladder."

"Then come with me."

His brows furrowed. "What?"

"Come with me. What's keeping you here in Mission? Beside your family, and your friends…okay, that is a lot to keep you here. But I'd like you to come with me and see the world."

"Get on a plane?" He pressed his hand to his chest and sucked in a breath, then another as he paled beneath his tan. "I don't know, Nic. What would I do? I don't think they have a need for ranching skills out in Paris."

"The world is an open book. We can go anywhere."

"A nomad's life?" His half-smile suggested her idea sounded as appealing as sleeping in the mud. "That's more your speed."

Pop! Any hope she had burst like a balloon jabbed by a nail. "Right."

They fell into an uncomfortable silence, each lost in their own thoughts.

Inside the house she could hear the clip of cowboy boots across the tiles, and the chattering of women, including her aunt's twittering laughter.

Out in the distance she saw a horse and rider approaching. Rafe on his black gelding. The unmistakable figure of Ben came out of the barn to greet him. From such a distance, Nic had no idea what they were saying to each other, but it had to have been humorous as Rafe bowed back with laughter as Ben rubbed his hands up and down the horse's neck.

The door behind the house slammed, then more voices trickled to where she sat. Happy voices. Warm voices. Caring voices. A family.

Family.

And maybe, just maybe, her family, too.

"I guess I could stay." Did she dare?

"How about option three?" Adam asked.

"What?" She turned to find him watching her with uncertainty shining in his eyes. And love. A whole lotta love. "Option three. Stay. Stay here. With me. Build a home with me. But take your trip to Paris first and…" He sucked in another breath and grimaced as if he was about to swallow a handful of worms. "I'll come with you."

"Really? Like, really, really?"

"Yeah. If you're willing to spend a second thinking about staying here for me, I can at least contemplate traveling with you. The way I'm thinking, we can have the best of both worlds. Would life as a part-time world traveler be enough for you?"

"More than enough, if you're by my side." She drew back and bit her lip. "Will this be one of those things where we say we're going to see the world, but then life gets in the way and it never happens?"

"If it does, you have permission to kick my ass. There is no doubt in my mind that in no time I will have a passport and you will see to it that it's filled with stamps."

"How about we ease you into it? Vancouver B.C. first. Then maybe Napa, New Orleans, New York, and then Paris."

He hauled her against his side and nuzzled a kiss against her neck. "You forgot Las Vegas."

"You want to see Vegas?"

"Nope. There's something I want to *do* in Vegas." His eyelids lowered to a sexy smolder and the corner of his lip curled with wicked intent.

"Learn to play craps?" He shook his head. "Flirt with some showgirls? I know, hit a swingers' club."

He snorted. "Not even close."

"Have sex in the middle of a crowded dance floor in a night club?"

"Ooo. Now that does sound appealing. But that wasn't what I was thinking. Here's a hint. We should hit Vegas first so you'll only have to get a passport once."

"Are you planning on getting us arrested to the point where I have to change my name in order to leave the country?"

"Just you wait, Nicolette Fournier," he laughed. "I'll get my ring on you yet."

"As proposals go, that was really lame, cowboy."

"Don't you fret, sweetness. You'll know it when I officially propose." He leaned in until their lips touched. "It'll be romantic. Just you and me, maybe a cheesecake or two."

He smothered her laughter with a kiss that was far more decadent and sweeter than any cheesecake ever invented.

Epilogue

"MA. WE'RE HERE," Adam hollered as he stepped across the threshold of his childhood home. "Watch your step there, sweetness. I've tripped over that door sill many times."

"Thanks," Nic said, peering around the heavy cakebox in her hands as she took a careful step over the jamb. This was her first family dinner with the entire Maguire clan in attendance and it wouldn't surprise her one bit if the jokester gods decided lemon icing would make a fantastic accessory to her wardrobe and have her fall into the five-layer masterpiece she had worked all of the previous day on.

"Uncle Adam!" came the shouts of several young voices followed by thunderous footfalls. Three boys skidded to a halt before them and fixed wide-eyed gazes on the numerous bags Adam held in his grip. "Did you bring us something from New York?"

"That depends," he replied with a narrow-eyed stare. "Are you going to give Nic and me a proper hello?"

As one, the boys turned to her and shouted, "Cake! Awesome! What kind?" and after that she didn't understand another word as they talked over each other in a cacophony of noise that convinced her on the spot that if she were ever to have children, they'd be girls.

"Never mind. Thank me later." He tousled each boy's hair as he handed them a bag. "Here you go."

"Is that my baby?" Beverly cried as she dodged the blur of excited children who took off for the family room in a whirlwind of energy. She wrapped her arms around her son, leaving prints in the fabric of his shirt with her wet hands. "I'm so glad you're home."

"Happy birthday, Ma." He raised the rest of the bags in his hands and waved them enticingly. "I brought you loads of presents."

"Your being home is present enough for me. Hello, Nic darling." She leaned around the box Nic carried to place a kiss on her cheek.

"Happy birthday, Mrs. Maguire."

"Thank you, dear. And please, call me Beverly. You know I consider you one of the family."

Nic smiled. "It's a force of habit from the shop, but I'll try. I brought you your favorite cake. Lemon chiffon with strawberry preserves."

Beverly closed her eyes and heaved a happy sigh. "I knew you were my favorite."

"Hey," Adam interjected. "I thought *I* was your favorite?"

"Son. You're my favorite son. Nic is my favorite daughter. And don't roll your eyes at me, Nicolette," she added as she turned away, taking the cake with her. "It's only a matter of time before you two are hitched. Mark my words."

"I wasn't arguing," Nic replied with a chuckle. She flashed Adam a wink before leaning over to brush his lips with a quick kiss.

His gaze traveled down the chain around her neck to where

it disappeared between the deep vee of her cleavage. The knowing light in his eyes warmed her more than the summer sun as a sparkle glinted against her breasts.

Just as he had promised, Adam had proposed to her in a much more romantic fashion than he had while they had sat on the swing of the Armstrongs' house. A week had passed, and they had been resting on a blanket, watching a movie outside in Bryant Park in Manhattan. The night was clear, and for once the light pollution was dim enough for her to count the stars. As Westley and Buttercup rode off into the distance on the big screen, Adam had leaned over to whisper in her ear, "Nicolette Marie Fournier. I love you. Will you do me the honor of marrying me and being my love for the rest of my life?"

The sincerity and love in his voice paralyzed her for several long seconds. How long had she waited to hear someone say those words? Declare their love and state their desire to build a life with her? The moment was perfect, and she had wanted to relish every second of the surprise for as long as possible.

In her peripheral vision she noticed the shiny ring in his hand as his arm wavered while he waited for her answer. He hadn't needed a ring. No, all she had needed was to see the besotted look in his eyes when she turned to face him.

"Yes," she said with the utmost conviction. "Absolutely yes."

"Yeah?" Relief eased the frown on his brow a second before she launched into his arms with a kiss of fire and passion she couldn't contain.

When she had pulled away to gasp for breath, he jumped to his feet and shouted, "Yahoo! This pretty lady right here just agreed to be my wife. Best. Day. Ever!"

Around them the other moviegoers erupted in applause and burst out into laughter as Adam dove on top of her and smothered any embarrassment she might have felt at being the center of attention with exuberant kisses. He had been right. Best. Day. Ever.

But they weren't ready to share their news just yet, especially since Adam suspected his mother would rev up the wedding train and have them neck deep in floral arrangements before they finished making the announcement. So for now the secret was their own and she kept the ring tucked against her heart. She had to admit, the cowboy had done well and had picked out the most beautiful antique ring she had ever seen.

"Hey." Adam's brother Angus interrupted their goo-goo eye session with a bellow and perturbed frown. "Did you just give the boys a cereal box-sized of Nerds and gummy bears as big as their heads?"

"Yep," Adam replied with a grin that suggested he knew full well the chaos he was creating.

Angus shook his head. "You suck, dude. But at least you only doped up my one kid and not Zach's two."

"Are you three going to stand there," Andrew asked as he crossed his path on his way to the dining room, "or are you gonna come eat?"

"Yeah, yeah." Adam waved him away. "We're coming."

After greeting the rest of the family, everyone took their seats in as organized a fashion as possible, fitting so many bodies around the long table. As always, a place for Adam's brother Scott was set at the table with a single yellow rose laying across the plate.

"Tell me, Nic," Angus asked as they dug into the feast of mashed potatoes and grilled porterhouses. "Did they have to tie Adam down to his seat when he boarded the plane? Did he cry like a little girl?"

"I did just fine," Adam answered for her. "It wasn't so bad.

In fact, I slept like a baby both ways."

Seated on her other side was Travis, who raised his brow in disbelief. "Really?"

"That's right," Adam said and bit into a chicken leg with gusto.

Travis caught her gaze and raised a brow.

"Really," she confirmed. "He did well."

"I wonder how he managed that," he murmured.

She tilted her head and whispered for his ears only, "Might have been that half tablet of Valium I snuck into his beer before we boarded."

"Genius, girl. Genius," he said with a chuckle.

"You know," Adam said as he reached the end of his tale of their trip to the Big Apple. "I ended up liking New York way more than I thought. Wouldn't mind going back. But I'm really glad to be home."

"Me too, sweet pea." His mother reached out and clasped his hand. "And what about you, Nic? Are you glad to be home?"

Whether Beverly meant to or not, she had asked the million-dollar question. After getting a taste of her former life, was it possible for Nic to be happy in Mission?

Around her were the people who would soon become her family. People who loved each other just as fiercely as they lived to annoy the hell out of each other. And back at the Sprawling A was an entirely different family, who were much the same way.

She took Adam's other hand and gave it a firm squeeze as she smiled up into his questioning eyes. "Yeah. I'm really glad to be home."

Do you want to know what really happened to
Scott Maguire?

Check out his story in Adamantium's Roar. Part of the Elite
Metal box set out now!

Elite Metal

Adamantium's Roar

*Adamantium left Beth to what he thought was a better life,
only to find she had been living in hell. Now he'll do
anything, break any vow, to claim her as his for all time.*

Adamantium feels right at home being back to what he does best
with his Elite Metal buddies, especially if it keeps his mind off
her. Beth Bradshaw. His best friend's girl. But when their paths
cross again, he discovers Beth is in the hands of a dangerous
man. Vow or no vow to his Elite Metal family, Ant will do
anything to claim the woman he loves.

EXCERPT

WAS HE FLIRTING with her? Her husband's best friend? The quiet guy who had always seemed to be more interested in video games and computers than women? Oh, he had had the occasional girlfriend, but never a relationship one would call serious, at least that she had seen. And he had never given any indication that he thought of her as a woman. As in a real woman. As in a potential mate and bed partner.

But there was certainly a vibe coming from him now. A subtle flex of muscles and a narrowing of his gaze that suggested he was interested in far more than merely reminiscing about the past.

"Here we go," he said as he steered the car off the freeway. Two blocks further down the road, he turned into a driveway of a motel. "We're already checked in and the parking lot is in the back, so we won't be seen from the streets. When we get settled why don't you take a bath, relax, and I'll get us some dinner and some shoes for you."

At the word "bath" she imagined being soaking wet and naked while Adamantium stood on the other side of the bathroom door in all of his manliness as he prepared to turn in for the night. Somehow she didn't think he wore pajamas to bed.

"Oh," she said and tried to control her racing heartbeat. "Um, sure."

Holy cow. Was she seriously getting turned on by her oldest friend?

"Sit tight here while I do a quick check around," he said as he parked the car. Once he climbed out, he stood by the side of the Charger. His tight backside was perfectly framed by the driver's side window.

She closed her eyes on a groan. Dear lord, she was.

ABOUT ANNA ALEXANDER

Anna Alexander is the award winning author of the Heroes of Saturn and the Sprawling A Ranch series. With Hugh Jackman's abs and Christopher Reeve's blue eyes as inspiration, she loves spinning tales of superheroes finding love. Anna also loves to give back and has served on the board for the Greater Seattle Romance Writers of America as chapter president and on the committee for the Emerald City Writers Conference.

Sign up to receive news about Anna's latest releases at http://eepurl.com/Q0tsz

Website

annaalexander.net

Facebook

facebook.com/pages/Anna-Alexander/282170065189471

Twitter

twitter.com/AnnaWriter

Instagram

instagram.com/annam.alexander

Newsletter

http://eepurl.com/Q0tsz

Also by Anna Alexander